ISIS ATTACKS AMERICA

BOOK II OF THE COLLABORATIVE SERIES
A CLINT BEAR NOVEL

Ken Berquist

I wish to express my appreciation to all of those of whom were helpful in creating this work.

To, Gail, my loving and very patient wife who understands, when I get into the 'writing mindset', it ultimately results in a periodic slippage into hibernation.

TABLE OF CONTENTS

CHAPTER ONE:
FRIDAY

The early summer evening was humid and still, with the outside guests' quiet conversations and intermittent laughing piercing the tranquil night. The patrons were enjoying the dimly lit ambience, the view of the starlit cloudless sky, and the five-star cuisine with expertly paired wines and attentive service.

The restaurant's garden wall that separated the New York City sidewalk and noisy street added a pleasant vista but did little to squelch the periodic taxi horn, noisy bus, and the sounds of teens riding their skateboards on the sidewalk. Still, New Yorkers, blind to the street noise, remained involved with their spouse, date, family or business associate, oblivious to even those seated at an adjacent table. The confused murmur of multiple disjointed conservations sounded like bees buzzing around their hive.

An elegant middle-aged woman was adding to the eloquent setting while playing "The Waltz of the Flowers" on a double-action pedal harp in the background.

They were among the lucky ones that had been blessed with a reservation at one of the top ten coveted "places to be" in NYC. Cecil's was a short walk from Wall Street, located in the first story of a converted brownstone with a private garden to its left, and a rear garden open for summer dining. All guests, as Cecil referred to his patrons, are met warmly and personally by Cecil. The parlor was flanked ceiling to floor with autographed photographs of famous guests, including the Mayor and Police Commissioner, as well as senators, F500 CEOs, the Vice President of the United States, Actors and Actresses, and many more attesting that this was, indeed, the place to be.

This Friday evening, among the many guests enjoying dinner in Cecil's garden, were Cole Cunningham, Director of Collaborative Field Operations, and his daughter, Beth, who was graduating with an MBA from Columbia. Cole spent as much time with Beth as his demanding schedule allowed since his wife, Jan, had lost her battle with cervical cancer just over a year ago. Cole was all too aware that he was a poor substitute for her mother, but Beth needed and appreciated his effort.

"Miss, may I refill your coffee?" the formally attired waiter asked.

Looking up with a broad genuine smile that radiated to all aspects of her face, Beth replied, "Yes, please."

"And for you, sir?"

"No, thank you. I'll nurse my brandy. You may bring the check any time, please."

Enjoying the calming harp playing in the background and taking a sip, nosing the snifter, while lovingly appraising Beth, Cole asked, "Beth, have you decided yet or are you still weighing your options?"

Beth coughed out a warm chuckle, nearly spilling her coffee. She was an attractive young woman who became beautiful when she smiled; it lit up her face, bringing her soul to the surface. Beth's eyes told of her intelligence, but they also reflected the street smarts learned from her years living in NYC. Her presence transmitted a directed, dedicated and determined young woman with the steel to back it up.

"Dad, I like the energy and the cultural diversity of New York, not to mention the opportunities available. But moving to D.C. would enable us to see each other more often, so I'm torn. Goldman Sachs has offered me a terrific position with a great salary and real responsibilities, especially for a recent grad. The World Bank's offer in D.C. isn't as much, but it would be more fulfilling. What would you think, Dad?"

Cole placed his hand over Beth's hand, resting on the white linen covered table, and leaning toward her and said, "Honey, you need to make this decision for yourself, not for me. If you're here in The City, I will visit as often as I can. If you are in D.C., we will see each other when I am not traveling for work and you'll have a house to live in so your expenses would be much lower. So, honey, think of…"

The spit from a silenced weapon made Cole abruptly turn in his seat, an instinctive reaction, to see three masked gunmen with assault weapons leveled at the guests. Turning back instantly, he watched as Beth's head snapped back, her forehead exploding in blood. Her eyes fluttered closed and her body slumped to the table before sliding to the floor, almost in slow motion.

Cole kicked his chair out from under him and dove onto Beth, shielding her from the now-continuous spit of silenced weapons. He winced as a bullet hit him in the small of his lower back while he was falling to shield his daughter. He consciously acknowledged that it felt different from the many bullet wounds he had suffered in the past, but he remained focused on protecting Beth.

Beth was unresponsive but breathing. Spit, spit, spit—the shots continued unabated, sounding like dozens of sprinkler heads watering a large lawn. Guests were screaming now, glassware breaking, tables falling over—all in what seemed like minutes but in reality was just a few seconds. Just moments before, father and daughter were talking about their future, and now Beth was in his arms, fighting for her life.

A cat-like scream came from further back as one of the bullets hit the harp and snapped a few strings.

Cole estimated that there were one hundred and fifty, or more, rounds loosed in this short time. He knew there was nothing more he could do for Beth, and drawing his service weapon from its holster, he became aware that his back was aching but he was entirely mobile. Odd. Perhaps a glancing bullet wound, he thought.

Turning slowly while jacking the first round into the chamber, he stole a quick look over their table to see each of the three masked gunmen dropping smoke bombs and then quickly retreating over the fence to the street. The gunmen were hidden in the smoke so Cole held his shot, for fear of hitting a pedestrian. He holstered his weapon and reached into his pocket for his cell phone, pressing a pre-programmed speed dial function key.

Something pulled at his suit jacket just as he finished his call and, turning, he became overjoyed to see Beth sitting up and wiping the blood from her forehead. As she did, Cole noticed there was no bullet hole, just blood. He gently folded her into his arms and whispered, "Are you all right, honey?"

Beth was confused, unsure of what had happened. Her vision was blurred and she had a massively throbbing head. She could see her dad's mouth move but the sounds were undecipherable, as if she were underwater looking up at her father speaking on the surface. There was a growing knot on her forehead that was excruciatingly painful to the touch.

Cole immediately recognized that she was in shock and beyond relieved she was not seriously hurt. He could hear police sirens in the distance, hopefully medical units as well. People began to help those that had been hit. He stole a glance around the garden and discovered it looked like a war zone, but yet there was something missing; something didn't fit. What the hell had just happened?

It came together for Cole as he reached for his back. The pain was definitely there but it was manageable, the blood evident on his hand but no bullet hole in his back. Beth's forehead was now smeared with blood, a large goose egg becoming ever more evident, but no bullet hole. These were rubber rounds filled with blood that exploded on impact, not bullets, Cole concluded. But why? It was a well-organized strike; military precision, stealth approach, fast strike, and organized exit. But to what end?

Beth was coming around now, frightened, shaking and sobbing, but responsive. "Lie down flat on your back, honey. I think you have a concussion but you should be fine in a day or two," Cole said as he was folding several cloth napkins to cushion her head while cradling her cheeks lovingly. "You'll have a hell of a bruise on your forehead, though."

The police started arriving along with emergency medical teams. Cole, leaving Beth for a moment, ran to meet them at the door, flashed his credentials, and quickly briefed them. "Make damn sure you take samples of the blood, and if any casings are found secure them properly as evidence."

What had been a wonderful evening for father and daughter had turned into a nightmare in a matter of seconds.

CHAPTER TWO:
SATURDAY

The next morning, Cole visited Beth in New York-Presbyterian Hospital and was relieved to see her sitting up in bed with a bandaged head. "Oh Dad, I am so happy to see you!"

"Honey, you have been through quite an ordeal. How's your head?" he asked as he leaned over the bed rail to kiss her cheek.

"The MRI the doc ordered confirmed your guess—concussion but no permanent damage. An inch and a half lower, and the bullet could have penetrated my eye and into the brain. The doc said that may have been lethal. He gave me something for the pain and my sight is almost back too normal. What the hell happened?"

A knock on the door interrupted Cole's explanation.

"Miss Cunningham, I am Detective Walsh, NYPD. Mr. Cunningham, I believe we need to talk. Take a look at this," Walsh said as he handed the Saturday Morning edition of the *New York Times* to Cole.

Cole froze in horror. The headlines said it all: "Terrorists Say Next Time Real Bullets." The story went on to say that ISIS had claimed responsibility, and their demands would be made in two days...and that there would be multiple targets across the United States if their demands were not met.

The radical Islamic State of Iraq and Syria was active on America's soil.

The news media had recognized immediately that the ISIS threat was a potential gold mine, and every newspaper coast to coast led with the story. The *New York Times* had the exclusive but the other major papers ran special editions, published by mid-morning, with expert opinions aimed to diagnose the how and why along with what may happen next.

C. Eric Douglas, former Director of the CIA, now Director of the Collaborative, was interested in only one newspaper, the *New York Times*. He was to report to the president in less than one hour and needed answers, and he needed them fast. He had ordered Cole to get to the newspaper's headquarters to get those answers, and then report back to him in D.C. immediately.

Cole arrived at the New York Times Building at 620 Eighth Avenue by taxi only minutes after talking with Douglas, having guessed his orders and taking the call while already en route. His credentials provided him with an immediate security escort directly to the Editor in Chief's office where the editor was waiting.

Paula Mitchel was standing by her door, having been alerted by reception that Cole was on his way. She was a news veteran, having started as a cub reporter thirty-one years ago. Her thick, silvery-gray hair hung to her shoulders and accented her penetrating steel-gray eyes. She was stylishly dressed in a dark navy pantsuit with matching low-heeled shoes, professional yet comfortable. Her eyeglasses were perched atop of her head with the temples embedded into her hair.

Extending her hand, she welcomed Cole, "Paula Mitchel. I'm happy to meet you, but I would have preferred it on better circumstances. Please come in."

"Thank you, Mrs. Mitchel."

"Paula, please. I expect we may be spending a lot more time together."

"Thanks, my name is Cole Cunningham, Director of Collaborative Field Operations."

"How is your daughter, Cole?" Obviously, the reporters covering the attack last night at Cecil's had reported that tidbit back to her.

"She is a still a bit shaken but she should be fine in a few days once the effects of the concussion subside. It was a bit scary for both of us."

While they walked to a conference table within her spacious office, Paula said, "I expect you need to know what *we* know…and this is the extent of it." She handed Cole a plastic Ziploc bag with a paper envelope inside.

"This letter came to me personally Friday evening, just as I was about to leave for the weekend. The envelope was touched by the receptionist, the worker in the mailroom, my assistant, and by me—no one else. I had expected that the NYPD anti-terror team would have been here before you, as the event was within city limits. But, given the content, it is clear to me that it is definitely a federal matter now."

Cole removed two latex gloves from his inner suit coat pocket, and after donning them on both hands and pushing each finger down tight, accepted the Ziploc bag. He opened the bag with care and removed the envelope, noting the inkjet print with Paula's name and title: *Paula Mitchel,*

Editor in Chief, New York Times, Personal and Confidential. There were no other obvious marks…but the lab might find something, he thought. Perhaps some prints or DNA on the envelope seal.

Then, with infinite care, he lifted the letter out of the envelope and unfolded it. The content was brief:

> *The Islamic State of Iraq and The Greater Syria has demonstrated our resolve at Cecil's restaurant. We showed our compassion for the innocent American people through the use of non-lethal means while demonstrating our capabilities. Unlike the President of the United States and his government, we did not kill innocent people, but this will change if our simple demands are not met. The president has five days to implement our demands. If he does not, we will initiate lethal actions across the United States, taking thousands of American lives, until he does. Our demands will be provided to the New York Times in two days.*

Cole read the letter three times hoping to uncover a clue, to no avail. Taking his cell phone out, he took pictures of both the envelope and the letter and attached them to a text message sent to the director. He then carefully replaced the letter into the envelope and the envelope back into the Ziploc bag, still deep in thought.

"Paula, there was no postage on the envelope. How was this delivered?"

"It was dropped at the reception desk in the lobby. Our security questioned the attendants and they said they noticed it on the reception counter, but didn't see anyone actually place it there."

"Do you have cameras focused on the reception area?"

"Yes. I will have security give you a copy of the video for the hour before the letter was discovered," Paula replied, picking up her phone to call security.

"Thanks. The demands they promise may be delivered the same way. I would like to post an agent where you have the security monitors as well as agents inside and outside with your permission."

"Cole, you know I don't need to give you permission, but yes, you have my full support. Thank you for asking and not demanding. It's refreshing."

"Thank you, Paula. That makes this simpler. I noticed that you didn't print the contents of the letter in your paper. Thank you for that as well. It may have caused wide-scale panic. Can we keep it that way in the future?"

"Well, Cole, I cannot guarantee that going forward. We are a newspaper and people have the right to know. All I can say at this point is that I will use my best judgment."

"That will have to do, for now," Cole said solemnly. "I will need to take this bag to our labs in D.C. Is there a private office where I can make a phone call? I need to brief the director."

CHAPTER THREE

Cole hated to leave Beth in the hospital, although she said that she understood and would be discharged in the next day or two. Beth was proud of her father but worried about the risks he faced every day in his role with the Collaborative. She had traveled extensively and therefore had firsthand knowledge of the dangers that every non-ISIS person faced each day.

The Situation Room in the lower level of the White House was crowded with the heads and deputies of the CIA, Homeland Security, the FBI, the State Department and, of course, the Collaborative. The president and vice president along with the secretary of state rounded out Washington's power team. The room was washed in overhead lighting, the air cool as was the temperament of those in attendance. It was the president that opened the meeting, "Douglas, what have you got?"

C. Eric Douglas was an imposing figure of a man and all in attendance were well aware that he was easily the most credentialed person in the room. His undercover and black ops experience in Vietnam, Iraq, and Afghanistan were legendary. Under his leadership, the CIA had regained prominence as the most effective intelligence organization in the world, something America had desperately needed.

"Mr. President, we have made progress in the last two hours but there is still far too much we don't know at this point. What we know is that there was a well-organized and well-trained team of at least four—one driver and three that accessed an upscale restaurant named Cecil's, in the Wall Street area of New York City on Friday evening, undetected. They opened fire on the patrons in the open garden using non-lethal rubber bullets filed with blood. The lab is working on the blood type and the bullet casings. There were no serious injuries, although fifty-three were hit resulting in broken ribs and arms, and head concussions. Among those hit was Field Operations Director Cole Cunningham and his daughter Beth, who remains in hospital with a serious concussion."

Douglas took a sip of water, allowing time for the attendees to digest the information before proceeding. Clicking the remote to show the letter and envelope on the high-resolution monitor, he went on, "This letter was delivered to the *New York Times* at approximately the same time as the attack at Cecil's Friday evening."

Everyone had stunned expressions on their faces, obviously reading the letter again and again for clues. But, there were few, if any, to find with the naked eye.

Douglas continued with the report, "The lab is working on the envelope and letter as well as the video coverage of the reception area where the envelope was dropped off. We have the prints of all *New York Times*' employees that had contact to crossmatch with any found. But, my gut tells me we will find none other than those belonging to the employees. My gut also tells me the print will come from a very popular inkjet printer that will be virtually untraceable."

The president jumped in, "Douglas, how is it we didn't know about this threat or at least have some warning that something was potentially happening?"

"Sir, there has been no traffic, internet or phone, that suggested anything. Our watch groups saw nothing unusual."

"Any idea of how ISIS passed our border security?" The president responded with some heat.

"No, sir. They could be sleeper agents. They could have passed through the thousands of miles of unprotected borders to the north or south, or the ocean borders, for that matter. Or, they could be pretending to be ISIS to cause widespread panic. We simply do not know at this point in the investigation."

William Thurston Covey, President of the United States, was not prone to overreaction. As a skilled Chinook chopper pilot with several successful wartime missions in Afghanistan, the last of which ended with him as a prisoner of war in a Taliban camp, he had learned to remain calm and to think under pressure. He finally responded with a question, "What do you think their demands will be?"

Everyone remained silent awaiting Douglas to respond. "My guess, assuming they are indeed ISIS, is they will demand an American withdrawal from Syria."

Every person in the room was aware that a withdrawal would be out of the question…way out of the question. Not simply because of the United States' hard policy of never negotiating with terrorists, but being experienced political leaders, they knew that success in Syria would save tens if not hundreds of thousands of lives, some American, some allies, and many indigenous to the countries in the region.

Most importantly, success in Syria would substantially stymie the ability of ISIS to grow and train their ranks, decreasing the muscle and reach of the jihad that has plagued non-Muslim, as well as Muslim countries, worldwide.

President Covey lifted his head and looked to Douglas, "Douglas, let's assume that ISIS is behind this for a moment. How large and well equipped do you suspect they are?"

Douglas agreed that this was a valid question, but he privately worried that his honest response would cause some concern and perhaps result in the Collaborative losing some credibility. He decided quickly that he would respond very carefully.

"Mr. President, we in this room know that ISIS sleeper agents exist in the U.S. We know that twelve thousand foreign fighters have gone to Syria over the last three years, about three thousand from the U.S., U.K., and France. The balance came from over eight-one countries. To date, eighty-two Americans have been accused of terrorist activities and based on FBI files, thirty-two have expressed interest in carrying out an attack on American soil, of which twenty-eight took steps to actually do it. Notably, two carried out the attack in Garland, Texas, but the two in San Bernardino, California, killed fourteen and injured twenty-two Americans. Most notably, a single man with an AR-15 killed fifty and wounded another fifty in the Orlando attack."

Pacing himself, Douglas took another sip of water before continuing, "We don't know the exact number of ISIS terrorists in America. My guess is that, if they are ISIS, we are likely facing a small team of ten to twenty at most."

"Okay, how well equipped?"

This question was easier to answer, "Mr. President, we can be reasonably confident that it is highly unlikely that they have radiological or chemical weapons, as they would have been detected when crossing a border or moving the weapons within America. Given the nature of the Cecil's attack, we need to be prepared for small arms and explosives that are readily available to anyone within America."

Letting that digest, Douglas then needed to put his last commentary into perspective. "Again, assuming this is indeed ISIS, we face a very formidable enemy. Remember,

ISIS is a political cult that has masked itself in a perversion of Islam. Think of it as a Hitler, a systematic effort to create a guerilla army of misled but very motivated followers. They expect to die, probably want to die; die as heroes killing infidels. We must remember the more recent incidents in Orlando, San Bernardino, Brussels, and France. A few people, even a single person with small arms and explosives, are capable of very significant damage to life and to a way of life."

The meeting was becoming more of a private conversation between President Covey and Director Douglas. The others were still absorbing the tragic information and thinking through the situation looking for options, when Secretary of State Elizabeth 'Liz' Madore asked the obvious next question.

"Director, how to we stop these guys? Multiple terrorist attacks on American soil would be catastrophic! Their success would provide a huge recruiting message."

Douglas had expected this question eventually. The occupants of the room were all focused on his response, looking for hope, a solid strategy and timeframe. He had always set proper expectations in a crisis, never over-promising results, and he wouldn't now.

"Madam Secretary, there are both short and long-term responses to your question. Let me start by reviewing the long-term, regarding how ISIS recruits on American soil. As we all know, they look for young people that lack direction, purpose, identity, and a sense of belonging to a cause. They find people that lack meaning in their life and who are disillusioned. They sell their solution; the fulfilment of being part of a battle that was prophesized some fourteen hundred years ago, to die as martyrs and be rewarded in the afterlife for fighting and killing the infidels.

Their recruitment message is, 'Join ISIS and the Muslim community and follow its teachings to earn the fulfilment you seek.' The long-term solution is to expose the ISIS prevision of Islam and the Qur'an for what it truly is by using American Islamic religious leaders speaking out publicly, and developing social programs that will provide the fulfilment directionless Americans seek."

President Covey had insisted that all White House personnel read the Qur'an and arranged for Islamic religious leaders to provide periodic in-house seminars in the hope that everyone had more than a basic understanding of both the Islamic religion and its twisted and perverted interpretation by ISIS. The long-term solution was, therefore, well known to the occupants of the Situation Room. It was the short-term plan that interested them now.

Douglas went on in his strong, motivational voice, "The short-term plan focuses on finding out who they are and where they are physically located right now, this very minute. The lab results of blood, casings, and paper may not help much because I believe we are facing a well-trained cell. We can hope to identify the person delivering the next envelope to the *New York Times*, and I have agents with video surveillance, both inside and outside the New York Times Building. We tripled the internet and phone surveillance in the NYC area looking for their traffic. This includes messaging platforms like KIK, Facebook, Twitter and ask.fm. All of our informants are being pressured for intel at this very minute."

Liz jumped in immediately, "Let's suppose we identify one of the cells. What's next, director?"

"We have a two-pronged approach. We will tag all their communications and in parallel we will infiltrate their cell. Their communications will help identify their numbers and locations as well as gain insight into their plans and timing. The infiltration will supplement and verify that intelligence as well as provide insight into the cell structure and capabilities."

Douglas let the room stew on the plan and took the opportunity to sit, suggesting that he was finished with his report. Clearly everyone in the Situation Room was aware of the seriousness of the threat, and no one offered suggestions or alternatives.

"Douglas, the demands will be published in two days' time. How soon do you expect to identify the cell?"

Again, he needed to set proper expectations. "Mr. President, that is unknown at this juncture. If we identify a cell member at the *New York Times* drop on Sunday, or intercept chatter, it could be fast—several days. If we don't, we could be facing terrorist actions on American soil. Our best early chance is identifying the person who delivers the demands to the *New York Times* on Sunday."

The groans and worried faces at the table conveyed real fear, exactly ISIS's intention.

CHAPTER FOUR:
SUNDAY

The soft patter of a light rain chilled the air and slowed the normally harried pace of NYC. The dark clouds prevented the noontime sunlight from penetrating the inner city, making it seem more like dusk. Pedestrians hustling to luncheons, shopping, and business meetings were shielded by umbrellas providing the anonymity that only one person sought. A slight breeze drifted, moving the drizzle at random angles and making the distant sounds of a siren from a fire engine or ambulance seem much closer.

A lone pedestrian was walking briskly south toward the Hudson River on 28th street, crossing 11th Avenue and turning left toward the old Terminal Warehouse. The drizzle was a gift from Allah as it kept most people indoors or in taxis.

The pedestrian entered the warehouse through a rusted gray metal door that squealed in protest as it opened, and then proceeded directly to an open freight elevator to get to the fifth floor. The elevator was noisy—a benefit—and slow—a liability—but there was no obvious activity outside or inside the building.

Lifting the expanded metal freight elevator door on the fifth level created more noise; squeaks and bangs echoed in the empty hallway. The hallway was dimly lit with incandescent lightbulbs hanging from the concrete ceiling by electrical cord, and devoid of activity, but that came as no surprise. Walking to the furthest door on the right, the pedestrian knocked three times on the metal door, waited, and then knocked three times again. A slot squeaked opened from within briefly at eye level. Black eyes peered out and then a secure bar could be heard being released from inside and the door creaked open. The pedestrian entered and the man inside re-secured the door.

"As-Salaam-Alaikum," the man said. *Peace be unto you.*

"Wa-Alaikum-Salaam," the pedestrian responded. *And unto you, peace.*

The room was small with dirty walls, and smelled of concrete dust and stale cigarette smoke. A single folding table stood in the room's center, surrounded by four decrepit folding metal chairs on which two young men sat quietly smoking. The only two windows in the room had been splashed with white paint, barely allowing the dim outside light to struggle inside.

Resting her umbrella against the wall, she stated, "You did well Hakim. Everything worked exactly as I had planned."

"Thank you, Amatullah. You planned the attack very well."

"Planning is important, but always remember, Hakim, that planning is based on assumptions…and assumptions can be wrong." Amatullah's dark eyes flashed under her hijab as she continued, "Planning helps prepare you and your team for the unknown. It is execution, flawless execution to achieve our purpose, that is important in attacks. And, you executed well."

Amatullah walked to the table while removing and draping her light jacket over a vacant metal chair, and greeted the two young men.

"As-Salaam-Alaikum." *Peace be unto you.*

"Wa-Alaikum-Salaam," the young men responded in unison. *And unto you, peace.*

Hakim reached for the teapot resting on the table and offered tea to Amatullah first, then to Tabari and Hanabali, finally filled his own cup before sitting. They sipped the black tea in silence, comfortable with each other's presence, the rain spitting on the panes of the two windows, the only sound in the room.

Amatullah, having finished her tea, addressed the small team. "You have done well, my friends. Allah, peace be upon him, is with us. Our mission is now underway and there is no turning back. Our people pray for us, for our safety, and for our success, as it will be their success."

She continued, "Hear me well. The next step in our plan is the most dangerous. The American people must feel the danger in their homes, businesses, on their streets, and in their public places. They must be in fear. The *New York Times* is the vehicle we need to create their awareness of our mission which will fuel their fears. For it is the American people that will pressure their government to submit to our will. Allah's will."

Looking at each of the young faces at the table she asked, "Do you understand this?"

Hakim was the first to respond and, as the operational leader, it was his place. "Yes, Amatullah, we all understand. The American people elect their president and senators, and they are the ones issuing the orders to kill our innocent people in Syria. We will, no…we *are* bringing their war to America and with Allah's blessing we will succeed!"

Tabari and Hanabali sternly nodded their agreement and crushed out their cigarettes in an already overflowing ashtray.

Amatullah nodded her approval and continued, "The next step is to provide our demands to the *New York Times*. It will be a letter in an envelope addressed to Paula Mitchel, Editor in Chief, just as before. We must assume that there will be FBI agents monitoring the newspaper, using every means at their command to entrap us. Therein lies our danger. We can't deliver the envelope as we did before. No one was aware of our actions then, but now they will be ready and we will not underestimate their capabilities."

Hakim gently asked, "Why can we not mail the letter or use a delivery service?"

"Hakim, this why I carefully plan our actions. The mail would not arrive on Sunday and we must be true to our demands by keeping our stated schedule. We have committed to make our demands known in two days from Friday, which means Sunday. A delivery service requires a face-to-face contact with the delivery company, and will increase our exposure and therefore our risk."

Hakim sighed in silent agreement while berating himself for not considering that, while Hanabali and Tabari listened intently. He privately resented Amatullah leading this cell, believing he should have that honor after recruiting Tabari and Hanabali.

Amatullah continued, "Tabari will have the honor of delivering our demands. But, since we assume the FBI will be there in force monitoring anyone entering the reception area, we will deliver our demands differently. Tabari, you will deliver the envelope inside the newspaper building, but not at the reception desk where they will be expecting you."

"I am honored you have selected me for such an important mission, Amatullah!" With a determined face Tabari added, "I will not fail you!"

Amatullah retrieved her smartphone from a pocket and fingered the soft keyboard.

ISIS demands that the United States withdraw from all action within Syria. The president will announce this decision within five days, and fully withdraw within thirty days. If the announcement is not made by a presidential speech, broadcast nationwide, within five days, Americans will pay the price. If the announcement is made but full withdrawal is not completed within thirty days, Americans will pay the price. ISIS has demonstrated our humanity, resolve, and capability without innocent deaths. Noncompliance will result in innocent American deaths nationwide, and the president will be personally responsible for the carnage.

ISIS 329HX56

She then sent the message to the wireless inkjet printer resting on the concrete floor by the inside wall. Donning latex gloves, as she went to the printer, retrieved the printed page, folded it, and placed it into a previously printed envelope. Back at the table she wet the seal by splashing the remaining tea in her cup onto the table and dipping the glue portion of the envelope into it and pressing the seal with her gloved index finger. Then she placed the envelope into a Ziploc bag.

Handing him the bag, she said, "Tabari, you will not touch this envelope with your naked flesh. Use these latex gloves when touching the envelope. I will explain to you privately, to compartmentalize this portion of our mission, how you are to deliver this most important message."

While Amatullah was whispering her orders to Tabari, several hundred miles south Douglas sat at his office conference table with Special Agents Clint Bear and Anne-Marie Meceli, and Cole Cunningham, Director of Collaborative Field Operations.

The mood was dark and the faces somber, but all knew there was no time for brooding. It was time for decisive actions, exactly where this team excelled. Just months before, this team had taken out the largest cocaine distributor in the U.S. with Clint working undercover as a Mexican drug lord.

Clint was dressed casually in blue jeans and a white cotton shirt. His shoulder-length black hair was pulled into a ponytail and secured with a matching black band. He had chameleon eyes, coal black set in almond-shaped sockets that could be soft and loving one instant, fierce and intimating the next. His prominent cheekbones were accented by strong nose and chin with smooth caramel skin. People that didn't know Clint gave him a wide birth, seeing a chiseled frame towering six feet two inches, wide at the shoulders and narrow at the waist.

Douglas started with his report. "As expected, we have little help from the physical evidence. The casings were devoid of markings or fingerprints. The projectiles were filled with goat's blood and I have a team of FBI agents scouring the area around New York City for farms where it could have been acquired. The few cameras outside Cecil's that could have provided video evidence were covered with black spray paint, which is too commonly available to be of help. The letter and envelope contained no prints but the seal showed evidence of tea leaves."

Clint jumped in, "Sir, it seems that we know very little at this point. What about internet and phone chatter?"

"Clint, we are monitoring everything within the NYC area. There has been zero related traffic before and after the attack. Zero. Remember, the chatter traps key words and phrases, so if they are using cell phones, email, or text they are being very careful with their terminology."

"So, that suggests the team may be relying on direct, probably in-person communication. What about video of the drop?"

"We have a slight break there, Clint. We isolated video coverage of the actual drop, but the guy had a hoodie with his face hidden from a clear facial-recognition shot."

"Sir, you say 'guy'. How do we know the dropper was male?"

"The lab concluded that based on walk, gate, and body metrics."

Meceli remained attentively quiet, as was her style, absorbing the intelligence or lack of it before offering comments or asking questions. As a veteran CIA analyst turned operative, she had an innate ability to parse information, connect disparate facts, and gain valuable insight that others frequently missed.

Cole added additional information as an eyewitness and victim. "Clint, this was a well-planned and well-organized attack. My daughter was hit point center in the forehead, an inch above the nose. These guys are well trained with solid leadership and discipline. Their attack was executed with military precision, in and out in less than two minutes."

Douglas then went on, "Our best chance for identification is the drop planned for today. We have agents outside the New York Times Building as well as inside the reception area. We have added video surveillance outside the building on all sides. We also have our people monitoring their internal video feed and we have added a few additional angles that we alone are monitoring and recording."

Anne-Marie Meceli was mentally placing herself in the reception lobby thinking through the drop, when a question came to her, "Director Douglas, what are the agents' engagement orders should they identify the dropper?"

Douglas nodding in respect, for the question was indeed critically important and one that he had labored over for hours during a sleepless night. He, and they, knew that there were really only two options—engage and arrest, or tag, if possible, and follow. Both came with extreme risk.

If the agents engaged and arrested the dropper, there was the possibility of suicide during the arrest, or the Collaborative agent's inability to break the dropper and learn the cell's secrets when in interrogation. Either way, the cell would know of a possible compromise which could alter their plans, perhaps accelerating their attacks.

If they were able to tag the dropper without being compromised, such that he thought it was a clean drop, they could follow him electronically for as long as the tag remained undiscovered. If discovered and if visual surveillance was compromised, all connection would likely be lost.

"I have weighed the options and believe a tag, if possible, and visual surveillance is our best option. We could arrest immediately, but with their demonstrated operational discipline, I suspect suicide martyrdom."

Clint Bear had been a behind-enemy-lines covert special ops expert in Afghanistan, with dozens of successful missions. Douglas had been his control and knew that Clint was the very best he had worked with in the military, as well as the CIA. It was Clint that immediately offered his commentary.

"Sir, tough decision. Either could work or blow up…but the odds, as I see them, are slightly better with your decision. How will you tag him?"

"With some luck we will be able to tag him twice. Since the *New York Times* published that their demands would be delivered on Sunday, it won't be unexpected that all people entering the building will be searched. Our agents will be in security uniforms. As we do the 'pat down' we will secret a Pearl, hopefully two. The Pearl is a sticky encoded transmitter about the size of a baby aspirin, has a range of sixty miles, and a battery life of ten days. The key will be identifying the guy first."

Sunday was a slower news day, but by no means a slow day. The *New York Times'* reception area enjoyed a constant flow of reporters, video crews, editors, and operations people. Even the credentialed *New York Times'* employees were searched for fear that credentials might have been compromised. With the exception of the roped off "pat down" queue, just after the metal detectors, all seemed business as usual.

Tabari had entered the New York Times Building through the revolving door off Eighth Avenue and patiently waited his turn through the metal detector. He was dressed in white pants, shirt, and tennis shoes, with a black stocking cap and a pale green canvas vest. He was carrying four large pizza boxes and looked like a typical delivery boy. His dark complexion, beard, and black eyes, however, immediately made him a person of interest.

Placing the pizza boxes on the table beside the metal detectors for manual inspection, his cell phone and keys in a small plastic tray, he walked through the metal detector without incident and waited for the pizza boxes to be opened and the contents inspected. The aroma of hot pepperoni pizza began to permeate the air, adding the needed credibility to his disguise.

Nervousness-inspired perspiration began to build on his forehead, armpits, and middle back. Fear choked his throat, for if he were discovered now he would die, but die a martyr. Yet, outwardly, he patiently waited for the boxes to be inspected, posing as a pizza delivery boy in no rush to return to the pizza shop.

The security guard then asked, "Where is the order for delivery?"

Reaching into the outside pocket of his vest, he removed an olive oil-stained slip and handed it to the security guard, saying, "Here, it is—four pepperoni pizzas for the auto advertising department on the fifth floor."

The security guard scrutinized the delivery slip and after determining that all was in order, he handed the boxes and plastic tray to Tabari and said, "Move on to the personal search station."

Relieved that they had not detected the envelope that was sealed in the plastic Ziploc bag placed underneath a pizza, and pocketing his cell phone and keys, Tabari walked the short distance to a roped-off area where two-armed security guards were waiting for him.

"Place the pizza boxes down and spread your arms and legs, please." Then one security guard faced him while the other went behind him, both removing the contents of his pockets, then replacing them and patting down his legs, arms, back, and chest. He felt as if he were going through a car wash or wind tunnel; his clothing, cap, arms, sneakers, and legs being frisked roughly.

"Okay, you are clear. Sorry to have inconvenienced you. The pizzas should still be hot," one security guard said as he waved his hand, motioning for the next person in the queue.

Tabari silently praised Amatullah for her brilliance. Her plan had worked so far, even though the most dangerous part was over. He was past security and now heading to the elevators. At the elevator bank he waited for an empty elevator, and once inside he pressed the fifth floor button with his index finger knuckle, just as Amatullah had instructed, to prevent leaving a traceable fingerprint. Once the door closed he reached into the pizza box identified by a small nick on the corner, removed the plastic Ziploc bag containing the envelope, and secreted it inside his vest just before the doors opened.

A reception area was located to the right of the elevator bank and he proceeded directly to the woman seated behind the desk. "Pizza delivery."

The receptionist gave a quizzical look and said, "I wasn't aware there was a delivery expected. Let me check." She turned and disappeared down the hall.

Tabari quickly opened the plastic bag and dropped the envelope into the basket labeled "Outgoing Mail" without touching it, and then looked quickly around to confirm his actions were unseen.

The receptionist returned with that same quizzical look on her face and said, "There must be some mistake. No one on this floor ordered pizza today."

Tabari feigned frustration and replied, "Not again! This is the second time this prank has happened. Bad for us, but good for you because you have four free pizzas! There's no point in taking them back, since we'd just have to toss them."

"Oh, I am so sorry for you," she replied with a smile.

Tabari retraced his steps to the elevator. After reaching the lobby reception area, he walked calmly out the revolving door, unaware that a hidden video camera within the elevator showed him removing the envelope, and that he had two sticky Pearls attached to his person.

A smile spread across his dark face showing his near perfect white teeth as he turned the corner, walking down Eighth Avenue and turning right on 41st street. Confident that he was not followed, he retrieved his cell phone to give Amatullah the good news.

***

Cole Cunningham, Director of Field Operations, was impatiently awaiting a status report from the team leader in NYC. When his cell phone rang he literally jumped, spilling the phone to the carpeted floor of the operations center.

Standing up and bending to pick it up, he said, "Cunningham."

"Cole, Russ Jacobs. We have good news and better news!"

"Russ, make my day, man!"

"We ID'd the dropper, a pizza delivery boy. Video surveillance positively recorded him with the envelope that was dropped into the fifth floor reception desk's outgoing mail bin. Better, we placed two Pearls, one in the lapel of his vest and one in his sneaker. Even better, we triangulated his location based a cell phone call minutes after he left the building, so we have his and what we believe is the cell leader's numbers and are tracking both now."

"Russ, you have made my year with this one! Okay, I know you, now give me the bad news."

"Cole, the bad news is exactly what you and the Director had expected. Their demand is total withdrawal from Syria. The envelope and letter are secure and en route to you in D.C., but I have an image being sent to your phone right now."

"Thanks Russ, and send my congratulations to your team. Keep up the phone and Pearl surveillance, and work to positively ID both the dropper and cell leader. I want to know what time and where they shit. Oh, does the *New York Times* know of the contents of the envelope yet?"

"No, not yet. We intercepted the envelope before they saw it. I'll call back when I know more."

Cole sat back down and processed the new intelligence. He exhaled a relieved breath saying partly to himself, "What luck!" Then he reached for the phone to call the team together.

The mood in Director Douglas's office had improved significantly with Cole's message that he was meeting them with an update. As Cole entered, he was greeted by Clint, Meceli, and Douglas. It was Douglas that opened the ball, "Cole, we could use some good news right now. What have you got?"

Everyone was standing, far too nervous to sit. "Sir, we have ID'd the dropper, secreted two Pearls on his person, identified his cell phone number and the cell of who we believe is the cell leader. Surveillance is continuing now to physically locate them using their cell phones as well as the Pearls."

The four of them then moved to the conference table to analyze the new information and talk strategy. They sat in silence as they each processed the intel privately.

Douglas broke the short silence, "That is the best possible news, Cole. Congratulate your team for me, especially Russ. Solid work. Now, what is the bad news?"

"Well, their demand is what you had thought it would be: total withdrawal from Syria, a nationwide address from the president within five days, and total withdrawal within thirty days. The envelope and letter are being couriered to the lab, probably in the air now. Noncompliance results in real bullets and American lives."

The air pressure in the room seemed to increase as they exhaled in unison. They all knew that the demand would not be even remotely considered. Not only because America would not negotiate with or be held ransom by terrorists, but because in all likelihood a withdrawal from Syria would result in far more innocent lives lost. The only option on the table was to take out all of the cells before the five-day time limit.

Making their task more demanding was the statement within the first letter that multiple U.S. cities would be targeted.

Clint was deep in thought, as were Cole, Meceli, and Douglas. The question was not just neutralizing the NYC cell now under surveillance, but how to get to the other cells. They had no intelligence to assist them beyond New York City. It was then that Clint formed the beginning of a strategy.

"I think we have only one plausible option; we must infiltrate the NYC cell quickly," Clint posed to the group.

Minutes passed as they processed the suggestion before Douglas asked, "Clint, you are the very best in covert undercover work that I have ever worked with, and by a wide margin. But successful infiltration within five days, no check that, probably within two or three days, is a very tall order."

They were all thinking the same thing, but no other options were tabled.

"I am making this up as I go, but we could use the model that got me into the cartel's drug operation a few months ago. We will need a way to make me very credible and very important…and very fast. My Arabic is rusty but passable, and I am dark completed so it is possible for me to pass as Middle Eastern, one of my advantages in being of American Indian heritage. It is the credibility…"

Meceli jumped in before Clint could finish, "I think this is a very good idea, Clint, and you don't need to be Iraqi or Syrian, you just need to be a devout Muslim. Look, we know that these guys are devout. Therefore, they pray five times each day. We know two of their locations, for now, based on their cell phones and the Pearls. What if we organize a sting and Clint saves one or more of the bad guys from arrest?"

Clint liked the idea as did the others, as evidenced by their nodding heads. They sipped their coffee and processed the possibility in quiet. The ticking of the wall clock was the only noise in the office and a reminder that time was their enemy as well.

Cole, as the operational genius in the room, had begun putting it all together. "I like the idea as well. The sting can work. We can save one of them from being arrested, perhaps both if they pray together. The credibility can be gained by Clint, after the save, indicating that FBI were probably after him because he has two RPGs. The cell would love to get their hands on them! Of course they will be duds, but they couldn't know that until they're used."

After a few more minutes of thought, Douglas said, "Okay. Work through the details quickly and be ready to brief the president in one hour. And Clint, this will fall on your shoulders once you have successfully infiltrated the cell."

Clint knew that what Douglas was really saying, was he may not make it through this operation alive.

To the north of D.C., Amatullah was in prayer, as were Hakim, Tabari, and Hanabali, all in separate locations. They had been instructed by Amatullah that their next meeting at the warehouse would be Monday.

Amatullah did not believe that the president would fall to ISIS's demands, knowing the hard line of the U.S. to not negotiate with terrorists. Therefore, Monday would be the time to prepare for their next action.

The President had a full schedule for a Sunday, so it was more than three hours before he could see Douglas and his team.

Clint spent that time thinking about his last undercover assignment, when his fiancée and sister had been captured, sexually abused, and then killed by the Peruvian drug cartel. While undercover, his father had died of old age and, later, his half-brother had died in his arms. The cost to him had been very high but the benefit to the American people was higher, with hundreds of thousands of lives saved from preventing the lethal White Ice drug from making it to the streets, and the elimination of the entire Peruvian drug cartel organization.

He thought of Meceli and how they had grown to care for each other. Or, was it more than that, he wondered? But it was too soon, with his fiancée, Brook, still ever-present in his thoughts. He concluded that he was still in mourning for Brook, coming to grips with his loss. Still, Meceli had saved his life, and he had saved hers that fateful night in Peru; they were connected now on a subconscious level.

Meceli, he was sure, felt the same connection. It was obvious in her smile and her touch, and her way of being there without pressuring him, giving him the distance he needed to mourn. Without having said it, she had communicated that she was there to help when needed, and wanted to be with him when he was ready.

Clint's thoughts were interrupted when the president's assistant said, "The president will see you now."

The team followed Director Douglas into the oval office to see William Thurston Covey standing in front of his massive walnut desk, dressed in khaki-colored Chinos and a navy blue Polo shirt, a reminder that this was Sunday.

"Douglas, I apologize for keeping you waiting. Issues of state, I am afraid. Please don't think that me not being able to see you more promptly implies that this terrorist danger is not foremost on my mind."

Then the president shook the hands of Director Douglas, Cole, and Meceli, before turning to Clint, "Nice to see you Clint." They warmly embraced.

"Nice to see you too, Bill," Clint replied. Since saving Bill from a Taliban POW camp some twenty years ago in Afghanistan, literally carrying him to the rescue helicopter and being shot in the back and leg in the process, they had developed a unique relationship. Clint was likely the only person ever to call the president by his first name while in the oval office, with the exception of his family, of course.

"Please help yourself to refreshments, and then let's sit so you can catch me up," the president said as he pointed to the service tray.

Now seated, Douglas took the next fifteen minutes to update the president on their progress.

"This is the best news possible…congratulations to you all. Of course, you all know that we won't give in to their demands and time is incredibly short, as I suspect is their plan. What do you suggest for our next move?" It might be Sunday, and the president casually dressed, but he was focused and very much on point.

"Cole, would you please outline your plan for the president?" Douglas passed the reins over to Cole, giving him command of the briefing.

"Mr. President, since we have tracked one of the cells and who we believe to be the cell leader, we believe we are in a very good position to quickly take out the NYC cell. Two have been tracked, leaving at least two, possibly several more, to be found. While we monitor them to uncover the rest, we need to think about the sentence in the first message relating to multiple American cities."

Cole then paused to sip the rich black coffee before proceeding, "In parallel with the surveillance operation, we need to infiltrate this cell to gain the intelligence needed to understand the extent of the threat, and if additional cells exist, locate and neutralize them."

The president's head immediately turned to his friend Clint, and Clint nodded his agreement. "Go on Cole, please."

"Our plan is to set up a sting operation where Clint is able to thwart the FBI's capture of one of the cell members and thereby establish his credibility. We will do this just following noontime prayers."

The president jumped in, "You aren't suggesting we invade a mosque are you?"

"No sir, that would be an incident unbecoming of the United States. We know that all Islam-practicing Muslims are not terrorists, but unfortunately a few are. We plan to have Clint in the mosque praying and after, while greeting each other before leaving, he will exit and immediately turn back in, saying that the FBI are outside. The few that follow him to the rear exit will likely include the cell member. As they exit, Clint will then apologize to the small group saying that the FBI are after him because he stole two RPGs. It is a gamble, but we suspect that the cell member will thank him for the warning. If he can engage and build rapport, he will. If not, he will leave and not push it."

The president remained silent, obviously thinking through their plan. "Okay, there is little risk that I can determine. What happens if he does not build the rapport with the terrorist?"

"Cole, may I?" Clint asked.

"Yes, please go ahead."

"Bill, you know that I speak Arabic and that my years in Afghanistan have given me a basic knowledge of many things of Muslim and Islam. If I can't bond with the terrorist after prayers, we think he will report back to the cell leader. We think that access to the two RPGs will be adequate incentive to find me. So, I will return to the mosque that evening and the next day in hopes of being contacted. By the way, the RPGs will be real but the grenades completely disarmed."

Douglas took this opportunity to summarize, "Mr. President, this is an unprecedented opportunity to infiltrate an ISIS cell operating on American soil. The intelligence we could gain, and the damage we could inflict with that intelligence is beyond anything we could have hoped for. This plan was conceived by Clint and devised by Cole and Meceli, and it is solid."

The president paused, processing all that he had been given and slowly began nodding approval. "Clint, are you sure about this?"

Clint remained still for a few moments before responding, "Bill, let me share a story with you. My father, Old Bear, as you know, was a Sioux Medicine Man and you may not believe in such things; but he had the ability to 'see'. He told me of the deaths of four family members days before they happened—Brook, Cabris, my half-brother Art, and himself. He told me of another vision; my purpose on Mother Earth. He said I had done well by the Indian people by building the American Indian Electronics Corporation, but that was not my true purpose, my destiny. It was far greater and it involved all people. He didn't know what that purpose was specifically, but he asked me to be receptive and available to it when it was made known to me. Bill, that purpose is to use the skills and experience gained while undercover behind enemy lines to help my country. Yes, Bill, I am very sure about this."

Everyone was deeply moved by the story Clint had just shared. Meceli, moved more than the others, dried her eyes discreetly.

"God bless you, Clint. America is in your debt again. Don't get shot because I won't be there to pull you into the chopper," the president said and then added, "Douglas, it is a go. Make sure the Attorney General has the needed paperwork and update me regularly."

"Mr. President, there is one more thing," Douglas added. "We need ISIS to think that you are complying with their demands. We suggest that you schedule a nationwide address for Friday, the five-day limit for the response. It may slow them down and we need all the time we can get. If Clint is successful, you could use that air time to announce that you have taken out the ISIS cell and possibly more, depending on the intelligence we gain."

CHAPTER FIVE: MONDAY

Clint, dressed in black slacks, an untucked shirt of white linen, and black sneakers, walked into the narrow entrance to the Masjid Manhattan Mosque. The unpretentious mosque was sandwiched between two bars with bright neon signs illuminating Warren Street, just four blocks from Ground Zero. Local residents, survivors of 9/11, and the family members of those who didn't survive protested its location, but religious freedom had ultimately prevailed, as it should.

The Pearl tracking device had had them to this mosque. Clint had therefore arrived late, and prayers were already well underway.

He removed his shoes and placed them neatly beside the dozens of others and found his way to a prayer mat, prostrated himself on his knees, hands outstretched on the mat, and began his prayers. He was just another devout Muslim now, but took every available opportunity to scan the room. What he was looking for he didn't know, but intuition had always told him to become familiar with his environment.

Clint had memorized the face of the terrorist that dropped the last message at the *New York Times* and knew he was here, but being late and now in the rear of the mosque, could not see faces. The voices of the Iman and those praying chanted, "Lā ilāha illā allāh"—*There is no deity but God*—while turning side to side. And then prayers came to an end with the fellowship and greeting, the congregation warmly and genuinely welcoming each other. A congregation at peace.

It was then Clint spied the terrorist and quickly made his way ahead of him as he went to the front door. Retrieving and donning their shoes, they made brief eye contact. Exiting the front door and seeing several black SUVs, he abruptly stopped and the terrorist accidently bumped into him from the rear. Turning quickly, he whispered in Arabic to the few congregants around him in the hallway, "FBI outside!"

Then he abruptly turned and started for the rear exit hoping he would be followed, and he was. The terrorist was close on his heels, walking briskly to keep up with Clint.

Clint opened the rear door slightly and peeked out, keeping up the ruse of the sting and then turned to face the terrorist, "It is clear, no one is out here. I am sorry; it was me the FBI was after. I stole two RPGs and they want me and the RPGs back. As-Salaam-Alaikum." *Peace be unto you.* And then he opened the door and walked away, alone.

Meceli was working with the lab, hoping to uncover some piece of intelligence within the letter or envelope, some hint as to who the other terrorists were. Becoming frustrated, she decided to check in with the DEA's Chief of Laboratory Sciences, now on loan to the Collaborative.

Dr. Kenneth Turner was, in a word, brilliant. He was as dedicated as anyone on the team and worked tirelessly to help the team succeed. If there was any evidence, no matter how slight, Ken and his team would find it.

Having cleared through security, Meceli entered the lab to find Ken hunched over a large microscope. "Hello Ken. I am hoping you have solved our mystery."

"Anne-Marie, I wish I could say that we have, but no…at least not yet. We have found the seal was again sealed with tea, and found concrete dust on both the letter and envelope, but that is it. No prints, no DNA. The concrete dust is old, perhaps seventy or ninety years old at least."

Dr. Ken Turner looked older than his fifty-five years. His gray-white hair was a mess, his pants rumpled, and his face drawn with black circles around the sharp blue eyes showing a lack of sleep.

Meceli recognized he was near exhaustion and said, "Okay, that is a good start. Now we know we are looking for an old building, perhaps unoccupied and dilapidated. You are beginning to narrow it down, Ken."

Ken added, "There is a reference in the letter that has us all buffaloed. It is the signature—ISIS 329HX56. Okay, ISIS we clearly understand, but what about the number and character string following?"

Meceli studied the photocopy of the letter and something registered, but she couldn't retrieve it. "It can't be a lat/long with letters in it. It could be a serial number perhaps, relating to their explosives?"

"We thought of that and did an extensive search with no results coming even remotely close. We are stymied, Meceli."

"Well, keep working on it. If it can be found, you'll find it. Of that I am sure, and Ken, don't forget to sleep," Meceli said tenderly, patting Ken on the back for reassurance.

***

The drizzle had abated in New York City and life had regained its harried pace. Taxi horns and diesel truck noise made its way into the fifth floor of the warehouse. The room was brighter now with sun reflecting through the whitewashed windows, but the stale air remained.

They were all sitting at the table finishing their tea when Amatullah asked Tabari, "Tell me everything that happened, leave nothing out. I want to know everything, every detail. Take your time. Tell me."

Tabari, concerned with Amatullah's wrath, sat nervously with Hakim and Hanabali at the folding table. "I had completed ṣalāt aẓ-ẓuhr, my noon prayers, and walked to the door, retrieved my shoes. As we all were leaving the Masjid Mosque, the man in front of me stopped very quickly. So quickly, I bumped into him. He turned and faced me and the others and said 'FBI outside' in Arabic and then proceeded to the exit at the back of the mosque. I saw a lot of black SUVs parked on the street just outside and panicked. So I, too, turned and went to the rear exit. It was just him and me. He cracked the rear door and peered out. Seeing nobody there, he opened the door and apologized to me, saying the FBI was after him because he stole two RPGs and they wanted him and the RPGs. Then he walked away and I did as well. That is everything, Amatullah, I speak the truth."

The room remained silent as Amatullah processed the information. She considered immediately that it was a setup, but to what end? Surely they would have simply arrested Tabari if they were after him. How would they have found him in the first place? Why wouldn't they have agents posted at the rear exit if they were there for an arrest? If they had identified Tabari they would have taken him, she concluded, therefore the cell must still be secure. It must have been the other guy they were after. Two RPGs would be invaluable, and she decided they must have them.

"Tabari, you have done well. I am convinced that our security is intact. Do you all agree?" She then looked at Hakim, then Hanabali, and finally Tabari, all of whom were nodding their consent.

"Good. I want to meet this man. Tabari, you will return to the Masjid Mosque for ṣalāt al-maġrib, your sunset prayers. If he is there, discreetly approach him…"

Cole's empty stomach betrayed the clock, telling him the afternoon was already upon him and the morning had vanished in what seemed like minutes. He needed to check in with his team and to save time, he invited Meceli to his office to get the report first hand.

"Russ, Cole, what is happening on surveillance? Meceli is here with me to save time."

"Hi Cole, Meceli. The two tagged phone people physically met, and then walked to the corner of 28th Street and 11th Avenue, entering a building called the Terminal Warehouse. There they met what looks like two additional people who were already inside, so we have no ID's. But, all four cell phones connecting from that location are now tagged. They are in the warehouse now and we have both electronic and eyes-on surveillance on the building. I am keeping our SWAT team on alert."

"Good job, Russ. What can you tell me about the two that you have ID'd?"

Russ, sighed, "That's the bad news. The phones are owned by a nonexistent company and the service has been prepaid for three months in advance. The second person was covering their face, and we still don't have a match on the first, so no results on facial recognition. They're ghosts, Cole."

Meceli surmised that it fit with their operational profile. They are smart, or at least the person running the operation was. But they are not *that* smart. If they were, they wouldn't allow their cell phones to be tracked this easily. Then another thought flashed like a beacon—maybe they want to be tracked, but why?

Cole interrupted her thoughts, "Russ, hold please while I patch in Clint."

Several dial tone bursts were heard on the before the speakerphone came to life with Clint's voice, "Clint."

"Hi Clint, Cole here with Russ and Meceli. Update us on your contact at the mosque."

"Hi guys. It went exactly as planned. I will be back for sunset prayers and my gut tells me he will be there as well."

Russ boomed in, "Clint, surveillance tagged your guy calling and then meeting with who we think is the cell leader minutes after your contact. We tagged another two phones so we are now following four terrorists. By the way, they're meeting at the Terminal Warehouse, 11th and 28th. My gut agrees, Clint, that they will make contact with you tonight."

Cole added, "This could be a banner day people. Stay sharp. Anything else?"

Meceli immediately said, "Yes," then paused before she continued, "The labs found old concrete dust on the letter. That fits with the warehouse. The envelope was again sealed with tea. However, they have no idea what the number and character string means in the signature of the demand letter, but they're working on it."

It was a balmy evening with a slight breeze from the east bringing the ocean's scent into the city and adding to the humidity. The sun had set and with darkness approaching, the city's underbelly began to awaken.

Intuition had rarely failed Clint. In Afghanistan, it had saved his life far too many times to count, even if he wanted to count those horrid days. Intuition had served him well again tonight.

The terrorist was following him out of the mosque, but had not made contact as of yet, so Clint walked a little slower to encourage him.

Finally, the terrorist came up beside Clint and said, ""As-Salaam-Alaikum," *Peace be unto you.*

"Wa-Alaikum-Salaam," Clint responded. *And unto you, peace.*

"Hello, we met at the mosque after noon prayers," he said.

"Yes, I remember well," Clint replied.

"I am Tabari," he said.

"Nice to meet you Tabari. I am Farel," Clint replied, offering his hand. "I was stopping for tea; would you care to join me?"

They entered a combination Bodega and café with a few small outside tables in a roped-off area on the sidewalk, and ordered tea. There was no small talk while they awaited the tea, which told Clint that this was a business meeting—they wanted the RPGs. Tea was served; it was weak, bitter, and horrible, but custom required the tea to be finished before they talked.

It was Tabari that broke the silence, "Thank you for saving me today."

"But, Tabari, it was me the FBI was after, not you. So, there is no need to thank me," Clint replied in a whisper. People were walking by, hurrying to their desired locations, taking no notice of Clint and Tabari.

Tabari was trying to set a hook but couldn't pull it off well, "Well, it could have been me, too."

"Are you okay? Can I help you, Tabari?"

"I would like to talk with you, but I don't know you. How can I trust someone I have just met?"

Clint thought, that's better, Tabari. Turn the tables and try to make me come to you. Well, it isn't that easy, son.

You must be what, about twenty-three, with no real experience, but I will play along.

"No, Tabari, you don't know me. I don't know you either. But, we are both Muslim and one of the tenets of our faith is to help our neighbors. So, I will help you if I can."

Tabari didn't know how to return that salvo and bungled the reply, "We want to buy those RPGs. Will you sell them to us?"

Wow, Clint thought, this kid is way out of his element. This is absolutely not how an ISIS operative would handle this discussion. Something is terribly wrong here.

"Tabari, slow down. Sell you my RPGs? And who are 'us'? Something doesn't feel right." Clint stood, placed a few dollars on the small table and added, "I better go now."

"No, no, wait! Wait…please. There is someone who wants to meet you and will explain everything. Please, it will only be a few minutes of your time."

Clint had stepped away from the table where Tabari was still seated. He half turned and gave the appearance of considering the request. Cabs, buses, trucks, bicycles, and kids on skateboards were busy all around him, the city now teeming with nightlife.

Clint sighed as if this was a big request and said, "Alright, Tabari, if this will be of help to you, when do I talk with this person?"

"Thank you, Farel. Tomorrow morning at 10 AM. Here is the address," Tabari said as he removed a piece of paper and handed it to Clint.

CHAPTER SIX:
TUESDAY

The 8:30 AM status meeting in the Oval Office started right on time, which was highly unusual. Douglas, Cole, and Meceli were there in person, with Clint and Russ by secure conference line. It was Douglas that provided the situation report for the president.

"Mr. President, we have been making excellent and continued progress. By triangulating the known cell phones, we have added two more to the surveillance and now have a total of four. We have eyes on them as well. Their base of operations is the Terminal Warehouse on 11th Ave in New York City. Their actual IDs have not been ascertained as yet, so they are not in the system. The phones are all registered to a nonexistent company and prepaid for three months."

"Clint, how did the meeting go last night," Douglas asked.

"Very strange. I am in, but not all the way yet. I meet who I expect is the cell leader today at 10, by Battery Park. And sir, something stinks. This doesn't feel right. The terrorist, his name is Tabari by the way, might be twenty-three and has no real experience. He could be ISIS, but why send a newbie on a mission like this? It just doesn't feel right."

Meceli agreed completely, "Clint, I have been having the same feeling. We're missing something important here."

The president was stroking his chin throughout this dialogue and then stopped, "People, we can't afford to miss anything here. Regardless of their experience, they have weapons and explosives and have committed to take innocent American lives. Twenty-three or eighty-three, we need to know who they are, where they are, what they plan to do, when and where!" Then pausing and rubbing his forehead, "Sorry everyone…you are doing terrific work and have made tremendous progress in such a short period of time."

Douglas closed out the meeting at this point, "Russ, keep the surveillance tight, and Clint, check in after your meeting at 10. And, Clint…be very careful."

Clint hailed a cab and provided the address, "Pier 15, Battery Park" and expected a lengthy ride from his location in Midtown. He used the time to reflect on what he knew so far and that uneasy feeling continued to burn like stomach acid. The ISIS operations had been expertly done, with the exception of communications and the meeting with Tabari. Maybe his meeting with this person would provide some answers.

Pier 15 was located on the East River side of the island and provided a grand view of the Brooklyn Bridge. Most of the pier was consumed by commercial interests, with only a few temporary slips available for arriving and departing passengers. The pier had been refurbished recently and the newly sealed planking was slippery with sea mist.

Clint waited patiently on the pier to be contacted by Tabari, realizing he was several minutes early. He watched as a sightseeing craft motored down the East River under the Brooklyn Bridge, and was surprised when it pulled into a vacant Pier 15 slip. It was a good-sized vessel, perhaps forty feet in length, with an enclosed wheelhouse forward of the rows of bench seats amidships and in the stern. Tabari was seated on one of the stern seats, alone, and motioned for Clint to come aboard.

Clint got right to it, "It would appear that you are alone, Tabari, so I will leave you to your sightseeing." But, as he was about to turn and leave, a tall woman stepped from the shadows and asked, "Please join us Farel. We have much to discuss."

The woman was in her late twenties, perhaps early thirties, with hair hidden by a gray silk hijab that accented her bronze skin and black eyes. She was dressed in a light black raincoat with black flat-soled shoes, but it was her eyes, both fierce and alluring, that told of sadness and caused Clint to stare.

"Well, Farel, will you join us, or not?" She asked again with a more demanding, less inviting, tone this time.

"To whom do I have the pleasure to speak with?" Clint asked, so as to not make it easy for her.

"My name is Amatullah. In Arabic it means…"

Clint cut her off, "The servant of Allah."

"It seems you are an educated man, Farel. Perhaps we can do business together."

The sightseeing craft left the slip and motored further down the East River toward Governors Island and then headed straight for the Statue of Liberty. Tea had been served by Tabari while Clint and Amatullah enjoyed the sunlight and crisp morning air in silence. Clint had far too much experience to force a conversation and waited for her to start the discussion, which she finally did.

"Farel, thank you for saving Tabari yesterday. He is a loyal servant, though not the most gifted," Amatullah said, looking out toward Lady Liberty while Tabari was in the galley.

"I apologized to him because it was me the FBI were seeking."

"Yes, the RPGs. A very handy weapon, don't you think?" Then she turned and faced Clint—Farel—directly, and said, "I would like to purchase them. What is your price?"

Clint leaned on the rail looking down into the blue-green water, churning from propeller wash, and then up at Liberty before replying, "So that is why we are alone on a boat, out of cell phone range, beyond prying eyes and ears. Very smart. But, the RPGs are not for sale, Amatullah."

She smiled, showing the most perfect white teeth while her eyes showed respect for the middle-eastern culture of negotiation. Amatullah was most likely Syrian by birth, but what brought her to America was still to be uncovered.

"Farel, what if I told you that money was of no consequence. Would the RPGs be for sale then?"

"Amatullah, what do you plan to do with these weapons?"

"That, Farel, is why money is of no object. What I will do with these weapons is of no concern to you; know only that I will use them to help my people. What is your price?"

"Ten thousand U.S. dollars…each."

"Done. When can you deliver them to me?"

"Today, this afternoon. I will show you how to use the weapon as well." Clint was certain that Amatullah was the cell leader, the intelligence of the cell, and it appeared it was well funded.

Clint briefed Cole while in the taxi, using carefully selected language to prevent the cab driver from understanding. His next step was to brief Russ and pick up the RPGs for delivery that afternoon.

***

Agent Anne-Marie Meceli had been briefed by Cole immediately after Clint called. She was on the *New York Times'* website checking the continued coverage of the terrorist action and the president's nationwide address scheduled for this Friday.

As far as she could tell, all the stories were rehashes of existing information; nothing new was being printed beyond so-called expert commentary. It was then that she looked at the URL in the browser and something within the deep reassesses of her brain made her pause. The URL was www.nytimes.com/interactive followed by a series of numbers and letters. She quickly retrieved a copy of the ISIS demands letter, deleted the numbers and letters within the URL for the article she was reading, and entered those from the ISIS demands letter and pressed enter.

The *New York Times'* headline read "US Airstrikes in Hasakah Killed 38 Civilians." Could the Cecil's attack be directly related or perhaps a retaliation, she pondered? Reading further, the article stated that the compound of former Syrian President Lu'ay al-Atassi had been taken over by ISIS and the occupants, loyal to the government, hanged and burned, including former President al-Atassi's son, Khalid, his wife, Alima, and their servants. The two daughters that were attending university in America were spared, but live in the horror of their family's massacre. The U.S. had then targeted the compound and leveled it, killing all ISIS terrorists occupying the buildings.

Meceli read the article again and again. Why was the cell leader pointing to this article? What was the connection? Retribution didn't make sense, but nothing else did either. She needed to get this to the lab, Cole, and Douglas…immediately.

***

It was a beautiful early summer afternoon with a clean blue sky puffed intermittently with cotton ball white clouds. A gentle breeze continued from the east, helping to lift the truck and bus diesel exhaust fumes above the street level.

Clint was carrying the two six-foot-by-six-inch square unmarked corrugated boxes under his left arm as he walked down 11th Avenue toward the Terminal Warehouse. He was still surprised and very curious as to why he had been asked to come here, what Russ had defined as their HQ. Tabari was an amateur but Amatullah was not, and she had extended the invitation and was waiting for him at the rusty gray metal door.

"Hello Farel. Come in, please."

Clint—Farel—stepped carefully through the door and waited for her. They walked side by side to the open freight elevator, entering and heading up to the fifth floor. She was dressed the same as she was that morning, only now the light raincoat was unbuttoned and flapped in the wake of her walking.

There was no conversation until she used a key to open the metal door on the fifth floor. As she entered, she said, "We are alone, Farel. You need not worry, and we need to talk."

The teapot was already hot. Clint placed the boxes on the floor and accepted her invitation to sit while she poured the tea. They sat silently while they sipped the tea. Clint spied the inkjet printer on the floor near the inside wall, and tasted the concrete dust in the air. Amatullah seemed anxious and began before the tea had been finished.

"Farel, you have a military baring about you; your posture and alert eyes betray you."

A curious way to open the conversation, Clint thought. "I was in the Navy for many years. In Afghanistan for most of those years."

"Ahh, that explains your Arabic. Are you a true believer, Farel?" Amatullah asked, her intense eyes locked on Clint's.

"The one and only god is God."

"A crafty answer, Farel," Amatullah said with a smile while nodding her respect. "Do you have family?" Amatullah continued, shifting the direction of their discussion.

"No. I did, of course, but my fiancée, sister, and brother were killed by a drug cartel. My father died of old age several months ago and my mother long before that." Clint knew that keeping his cover as accurate as possible without betraying his true identity was always the best approach.

"So you know of the sorrow that cannot be healed. I, too, have lost my family...except for a younger sister, Aludra."

Amatullah seemed miles away with unfocused eyes and shallow breathing, but eventually returned to the present and said, "I have prayed on this and believe I should trust you. In truth, I have no choice. My life and the life of my sister Aludra are in your hands, Farel. I need your help."

Alarmed and a bit shocked, Clint had not been expecting a conversation like this but experience had taught him to flow with the present environment and he would do so again now. "Amatullah, I don't understand."

"Farel, my sister has been abducted by ISIS and in exchange for my leadership of this cell, she is being kept from the camps—the sex slave camps. If I fail, she will be lost—the only family I have left in this world. I believe you are FBI and your name probably isn't Farel. And, if I am correct, those two RPGs are probably tagged and definitely not functional. I pray that all of my assumptions are correct."

Clint knew he was in uncharted territory now. This could be a test or a setup that could get him killed, but intuition told him she was being truthful. Time was his enemy as well, so he must make up his mind now and ask Douglas for forgiveness later. He decided to trust his intuition.

"Why did you use non-lethal bullets at Cecil's?" Clint asked, confirming her assumptions without confirming outright.

"I was severely reprimanded for not killing all patrons at that restaurant, but I could not be responsible for taking the lives of innocent people. I am a devout Muslim and believe in the Islamic teachings of peace. But come Friday, it will be out of my hands, my sister will be gone, and I will likely be in the camps for not obeying ISIS orders. Please help me!" She began to weep, slowly at first and then uncontrollably, her hands shaking so fiercely it seemed she was slapping her face as opposed to dabbing at the rivers of tears flowing from her sad eyes. The enormous stress she had been carrying had finally bubbled over uncontrollably.

Clint thought that either she was an Academy Award-winning actress or that she was being truthful, and intuition told him she was being truthful. He immediately conceived of a path that would both help the United States as well as Amatullah.

"Amatullah, your assumptions are indeed correct. The RPGs are tagged and the explosives have been removed—they are completely harmless. Tell me what this all about and we will find a way to help."

"Thank you, more than you can possibly know. You are not Muslim, are you?"

"No, I am not. My name is Clint and I am American Indian."

"Thank you for your trust, Clint. This is what I know. There are five ISIS cells in America; NYC of course, D.C., Kansas City, Costa Mesa, and Boise—all are small cells, probably with no more than five people. The simultaneous attacks are planned in those areas but I am without details, as the details for the attacks in the other areas have been compartmentalized by ISIS leadership. The NYC attack is to be made on the Richard Rogers Theatre, where the musical Hamilton is playing, at seven o'clock. It is meant to be a political statement as well as a terrorist action." She seemed to be unloading without breathing, desperate to find a way out of this mess, feeling that sharing everything she knew would lighten her burden.

Clint consumed the new and valuable information and cataloged it for reference later before asking, "Why is ISIS forcing you to do this, Amatullah?"

"There are few in ISIS that are well educated, that can think and plan, and they know that I have that skill." She laughed sadly before continuing, "I never thought that graduating top of my class at Columbia would be a curse, but lately it has been a complete nightmare."

"And, Aludra?"

"She was attending Columbia as well, undergraduate in business, until she was abducted by ISIS nineteen days ago. We share an apartment and when I came home, I found a video queued on my computer with her bound and gagged, and two hooded men telling me what I must do if I wanted to see her again. It was terrifying for me and probably more so for Aludra! I was to be contacted by Hakim, a young man already in the NYC cell."

"Amatullah, are you being watched or monitored?"

"I don't think so…although Hakim, the operational leader of this cell, may be in communication with the ISIS leader in America. Hakim recruited the two others in this cell. The leader is located in Washington D.C., I think, but I do not know his name."

"Where are the RPGs to be deployed?"

"In D.C. They want them as soon as I make the purchase. Oh, here is the twenty thousand dollars," Amatullah said, as she reached into her purse and retrieved an envelope. "They wanted me to recruit you if I was confident that you were a devout Muslim, one of 'us', he said."

Clint needed to strategize with his team—this new intelligence was explosive, but he must keep connected to Amatullah to support her as she was close to a total collapse with such a burden.

Reaching for Amatullah's hands and folding them gently within his, Clint said, "Okay. Here is what you need to do now. First, know that you can trust me, not because I am FBI but because I commit to you and God that I will help you and do all within my power to get your sister back, safely. Second, when you leave here, go to an electronics store and buy a burner phone then call me with that cell phone number. Here is my cell number," Clint wrote the number on the palm of her left hand.

Clint then continued, "Next, I will meet with my team and devise a strategy and call you back on the burner phone later today. Tell no one of our discussion, no one. Lastly, you have recruited me, Farel, and introduce me to your team when you meet next and use only that name. Oh, and keep the money, you may need it later. Understood?"

"Understood. I thank God that you have come into my life! You have given me hope."

Douglas, Meceli, and Cole had received the text from Clint to be ready for a video conference call as soon as he reached the Collaborative's headquarters in New York City. They were pacing the floor of Douglas's office when his computer beeped, and he immediately switched it to the large high-resolution video monitor near the conference table.

"Douglas here, along with Cole and Meceli."

"Hi, I am here with Russ and we have a great deal to cover in a short time. First, the cell leader here met me and purchased the RPGs and she has recruited me. Second, her name is Amatullah, twenty-eight to thirty years of age, graduate of Columbia with a PhD. Third, she is being forced to do ISIS's will. Her sister has been abducted, her only living family, and will be sent to the sex camps if she fails. Fourth, there are five small cells operating in America: New York City, D.C., Kansas City, Costa Mesa, and Boise. Fifth, she thinks I am FBI and has asked for our help. Sixth, she disobeyed ISIS orders and used non-lethal rounds at Cecil's because she would not have innocent lives on her hands, and ISIS's leadership was not pleased. Seventh, she has pledged her full support to stop these attacks. Eighth, I have pledged my support and our support in getting her and her sister to safety."

Meceli jumped in, "That was why she sent that link! Oh, remember the character string following the signature in the demands letter? I found it led to a *New York Times'* article about ISIS killing the former Syrian president's son and wife. It also mentioned that his two daughters were attending Columbia. Their names are…"

"Amatullah and Aludra," Clint stated, interrupting Meceli.

"That's right! So Amatullah is on our side."

"No doubt about it. She has purchased a burner as I suggested so we can keep this compartment tight," Clint replied.

Cole asked, "Do we know where the RPGs are destined?"

"Yes, D.C. And, by the way, Amatullah is very bright. She surmised that they were tagged and disarmed," Clint responded.

Clint had dumped a ton of information and the team needed some time to process it. The long period of silence was finally broken by Douglas, "I assume you have broken your cover and I know you wouldn't do that without being sure of Amatullah's sincerity, so good work, Clint. We need to get the cell phone number of the ISIS leader in D.C. to Russ for surveillance. Ideas?"

"Yes, Director, I have been thinking about that. Amatullah will need to update him with the RPG acquisition and my recruitment status. Russ can tag the cell then, this evening. Since he wants them in D.C., I will suggest to Amatullah that she order me to deliver them, in person."

Cole jumped in, "Too risky, Clint. This guy is probably ISIS trained and, if so, he may make you as a Fed. How about that kid, Tabari? Can he make the delivery? We still have his cell and the Pearls to follow him."

Douglas was using his waving hands in a gesture for everyone to slow down and let him think. The ISIS commander in America was the single link to all the cells and to the ISIS headquarters, probably in Syria. He was the key conduit, the jewel, and if captured could reveal everything with the right interrogation techniques. How to do it? What was the best course of action? If he was neutralized would that stop the attacks? He surmised probably not, but at least it might cause a delay and give them more time.

Then Douglas came back to life, "Clint, have Amatullah make the call on her cell at five tonight. Russ, be ready to tag his cell. Clint, have Amatullah instruct Tabari to deliver the RPGs tomorrow morning by car, and Russ, keep the Pearls recording and immediately forward the location to Cole. Cole, you and Meceli work the plan to take this guy when he is alone. We want him alive for immediate interrogation. Questions?"

"Yes, Director," Russ said. "Do we continue to keep eyes on Tabari all the way to D.C.?"

"Yes, Russ, but with your best team. We absolutely cannot be made."

"Okay. He will need to have an address for the drop and that will likely come from the cell phone conversation. I will alert you all with that as well."

"If nothing more, I need to brief the president. Good work, team. Out."

CHAPTER SEVEN: WEDNESDAY

Darkness was giving way to an overcast morning as the marine layer began to magically disappear, radiated by the first beams of sunlight. Two agents sat sipping hot black coffee in a white nondescript sedan a block away from the Terminal Warehouse. They secretly watched as a blue Toyota Corolla stopped by the rusty gray metal door.

The driver put on the emergency flashers and disappeared into the building, only to return a few minutes later with two six-foot-long unmarked corrugated boxes, which were placed on the rear seat. Back in the driver's seat, flashers off, he sped carefully away.

The passenger agent lifted his cell and said, "Package on the way."

Several blocks to the north in the Collaborative's New York headquarters, Russ received the message and turned to the surveillance team and said, "Do not lose them."

It would be at least four to five hours before Tabari reached the drop location and all they could do now is surveil, wait, and pray.

***

Cole and Meceli were watching the drop address that the surveillance team had acquired from the cell phone discussion. Now that they had the cell phone under surveillance, Russ was providing regular updates on the ISIS commander's location. They had what they hoped was his home as the first location to assess for a stealth abduction.

The ISIS commander's phone had been stationary all evening in an apartment building on D.C.'s Kansas Ave, and the drop was arranged about two miles to the west in a Rock Creek Park rest area. They surmised it was selected as it was convenient for him. The question was, would he return to his apartment or go to his cell location? They needed to plan for both contingencies.

In the end, Cole and a team would enter his apartment after he left. They would secure any remaining occupants and await word from the surveillance team. While waiting, they would search the premises carefully.

Meceli and a second team would stand by in case he decided to make his way to the cell location with eyes-on surveillance. They would not take him there, but would wait for him to leave, hopefully alone. If he was alone when returning to his car, they would take him then. If not, they would wait until he returned to his apartment. The key was to take him alive without detection.

Tabari's eyes-on surveillance was challenged by his very slow and cautious driving but helped by the clear sunny day. On Interstate 95 South, he never exceeded fifty-five miles per hour. The agents actually worried that he might be pulled over by state police for driving too slow. The slow commuting traffic helped in some areas and they stayed well back out of detection range, aided by the mobile Pearl tracker.

The trip was nearing the end, more than five hours of driving, as Tabari turned off of Route 495 onto Route 29, heading south and west toward Rock Creek Park in D.C. The traffic was sparse on this rural route at midday so the agents distanced themselves even further. Then, Tabari, probably aided by his GPS, turned right onto Military Park NW and entered Rock Creek Park heading to the rest area by the public golf course. He pulled into the rest area and stopped, but the agents continued on past the blue Toyota Corolla and into the golf course parking lot a short distance further where Meceli and her team were standing by. The agent in the passenger's seat lifted his cell, "Package stopped in the rest area, awaiting the meet and pickup."

There were six agents secreted in the wooded areas surrounding the rest area. Their job was to observe and report only, not to be seen or interact.

Minutes later, a black mid-sized Land Rover with tinted windows pulled into the rest area and stopped directly beside the blue Corolla. No more than four feet separated the vehicles. No one exited either vehicle. Tabari looked to be on his cell, but person in the Land Rover was still unknown, hidden by the tinted windows.

Then Tabari got out of the Corolla, opened its rear door, and removed the two boxes containing the RPGs. He then turned and opened the Land Rover's rear passenger door, placed them on the seat, and closed its door. The Land Rover then pulled slowly away continuing its direction of travel and Tabari got in the Corolla and made a U-turn, apparently heading back to New York following the same route that brought him here.

One of the agents observing had a view into the Land Rover when the rear door opened and confirmed that there was a single occupant—the driver.

*****

Earlier, Cole's team had taken the apartment using the superintendent's key to open the door. Cole was surprised to find a wife and two daughters, both in their early teens. They were immediately taken to a Collaborative detention facility in D.C. and separated, while they awaited interrogation.

The team then settled in, waiting for the ISIS commander to return home, confident that the surveillance team would alert them well before his arrival. While waiting they searched the house, as planned, and found three notebook computers and a satellite phone, but nothing else of interest.

So, they now sat and waited. When the surveillance team notified Cole that their target was due to arrive, he would post two agents outside, secreted in the parking lot, two in the apartment hallway janitor's closet, and three in the apartment itself. There would be no chance the ISIS commander could flee, and the takedown would be too fast for a suicide attempt.

Director Douglas's orders were firm and clear, "Take him alone and take him alive."

Eyes-on surveillance of the commander now equated to eyes on the mobile Pearl tracking device monitor as they were concerned about detection from a more experienced ISIS operative. The Pearls that had been inserted into both RPG shoulder stocks were transmitting perfectly.

The black Land Rover continued on Military Road NW, and then circled around and made its way onto Morrow Drive NW across 16th Street and onto Kennedy Street NW, heading east directly to Kansas Avenue NW, where his apartment was located. The surveillance team pinged Cole and he got his welcome party in place.

They had set up a video feed of the apartment complex parking lot, and several minutes later Cole watched as the black Land Rover pulled in and parked near the rear entrance to the building. The tinted windows prevented the video coverage from seeing who was inside, but then the driver's door opened and a tall well-dressed man stepped out. He was dressed in a beige suit, an open-collared white shirt, with black hair and a full but trimmed black beard.

The ISIS commander briefly canvassed the surrounding area and, apparently satisfied there was nothing unusual, walked into the building using his remote to lock the vehicle. A few short minutes later, he inserted his key into the apartment door deadbolt and turned the doorknob. An explosion of activity ensued when Cole aggressively pulled the door open, gun in his right hand, and two agents securing the ISIS commander's arms from behind with zip ties.

Looking at him with angry eyes, Cole spat, "You are under arrest as a prisoner of war." Then a hood was placed over the man's head and pulled tightly around his neck.

He was screaming for his wife and daughters when the hypodermic needle entered his arm, and within seconds he slumped toward the floor as he lost consciousness. A gurney was then wheeled into the apartment and two agents lifted him to its surface, replacing the zip-ties with handcuffs, secured both arms and both legs to the gurney's metal rails. Then they pulled a white sheet completely over his body and headed to the elevator where a nondescript ambulance would be waiting at the basement exit.

Two agents left from the side entrance with the Land Rover's keys, a 9mm Glock, and his cell phone that had been retrieved after the commander lay unconscious. Cole then updated Douglas, informing him that the team and package were en route. Meceli, hearing the situation report, ordered her team to stand down and head back to HQ as well.

The ISIS commander had been taken alone and alive. The director would be pleased.

The center of focus was now in Washington D.C., with the commander's interrogation and the dump of his cell and satellite phones, and it needed to start immediately. The phones were delivered to Ken Turner's lab with maximum priority. The sedative given to the commander was both fast acting and quick to dissipate, and he was fully coherent when the ambulance arrived at the Collaborative HQ.

Clint was updating Amatullah on her burner but left the facts at a high level. "Amatullah, we have the ISIS commander in custody and will begin interrogating him within the next hour. We have his cell and satellite phones as well, and hope to locate the other cells by the end of the day. Please stand down until you hear from me later today or tomorrow. I will try to determine where your sister Aludra is—keep praying."

"Thank you so much, Clint! May God and speed be with you."

Douglas had amassed his small team in a secure basement room two doors down from the interrogation room. Meceli and Cole were anxiously awaiting his instructions. There was a video feed from the interrogation room displaying on the high-resolution wall-mounted monitor. The commander sat, cuffed to a robust metal chair that was bolted to the floor, with one agent standing inside the door.

"Meceli, I want you to initiate the interrogation. You have done this many times, so you know the technique. As a woman—specifically a woman in charge—since he is a Muslim, he will feel humiliated and will likely not be immediately communitive. We need to know the location of the five cells but don't let on that we know about the New York cell. And, we need to know his reporting structure. Are you ready?"

"Let's do it, Director."

Meceli left the room, stopped in the hallway, and took a few deep breaths to quiet her mind. She knew she had leverage and focused on the important opening questions. The way she opened would determine her success. Then she snapped the door handle, intentionally making a jarring sound, and entered the interrogation room with speed, authority, and stature.

Meceli was dressed in a black pantsuit, white-collared blouse and black, flat, rubber-soled shoes. She looked as professional as she was competent. Her shoulder-length chestnut hair was pulled back into a ponytail. Entering the room, she focused on his eyes with a penetrating and confident stare. Without breaking eye contact, she waved her hand to dismiss the agent, saying, "Leave us, please." The agent left without responding, quietly closing the door behind him.

She walked to him, keeping eye contact until she walked past the chair on his left, circling around him until she faced him again. There is a maxim that "the first to speak loses" and she knew it well. It was very appropriate for interrogations.

He spat out, "I want my lawyer and I will give you nothing."

Meceli left his demands hanging in the stale air for a moment before responding, "You are a terrorist and a prisoner of war. You have no rights and you will see no lawyer, now or ever. You have two options; life in prison or death. Personally, I am hoping for your death, and the slower and more painful it is the more I will like it."

He sat, eyes wide and darting about the room while he tried to piece together his options. Perspiration began showing on his forehead and his tongue tried in vain to wet his lips.

"What have you done with my family? They have done nothing!" he demanded.

"What have you done?" Meceli responded in a conversational tone, purposely not responding to his question, keeping the initiative and control.

"I have done nothing!" he screamed.

"Oh, but you have. We have been watching you for weeks. Your cell phone provided us with all we need."

"You lie, bitch! My cell phone was secured." He replied, snickering.

"You are a fool. We bypassed your phone security in a matter of minutes." Meceli said not letting him win a salvo.

Minutes passed silently. The commander was lost in thought, concerned for his family and confused as to how he was caught. What was to be a big day for him had turned to a nightmare beyond his comprehension.

"What have you done with my family?" he asked in a more controlled tone, breathing out a long breath.

"They have been arrested as well. You know what ISIS does with American girls? Well, we know…and maybe we should do the same with your family!" Meceli spat out viciously.

"You wouldn't dare do that, not the United States!"

"So, you admit you are ISIS. That is a start."

"I did not say that, you tricked me!"

"What do you think will happen to your family when ISIS in Syria learns that you have admitted you are ISIS, and operating here in America? Well? Maybe we won't need to do anything; they will take care of your family problem for us and our hands will be clean. They do need to set an example now and then, don't they?" Meceli asked with a smirk on her face while staring directly at the commander.

He sat, head down, shoulders rolled over, emotion and exhaustion taking their toll as he thought that this wasn't how he'd expected this day to unfold when he had kissed his lovely wife and daughter's goodbye this morning.

"Would you like water?" Meceli said, sensing that he was on the verge of breaking.

"Yes."

"I will have a bottle of water brought in and will un-cuff your left hand. But first, I will make one offer, the only offer you will get to save your family. Hear me well as this will be the only offer. Do you understand?"

Minutes passed as he struggled to find an alternative where there was none, and finally responded to Meceli's question, "Yes."

"Good. The offer is this: we will leak a story to the press that you were shot and killed during an arrest. This will clear your family from ISIS retribution. In return, you will answer every question we ask, truthfully. If we find that you have not answered a single question fully and truthfully, even to omit the smallest of details, we will not leak the story to the press. On the contrary, our press release will indicate that you have talked freely telling us everything we wanted to know, and your wife and daughters will be released and pay the ultimate price with their lives. It won't be quick and it won't be pretty, as I am very confident you know. Understood?"

His eyes closed and he exhaled deeply. Then, he lifted his head and said in a whisper, "Yes."

Meceli motioned to the room's camera and microphone, "Please bring in a bottle of water for…what is your full name…?"

Douglas and Cole were watching the interrogation on the monitor when Cole said, "She is masterful. I am very happy she is on our team. Standard techniques could have taken hours or days, but she used his family as his Achilles' heel and cracked him in less than thirty minutes."

Clint had taken a military transport directly to D.C. and was in Douglas's office with Cole and Meceli for the situation report later that day.

Douglas started the meeting, "We are in field goal range but not in the red zone yet. Ken has dumped the cell phone but we're still working on the satellite phone and we have surveillance on the other cell leaders. Cole, you will coordinate multiple synchronized takedowns at oh-dark-thirty Friday morning. When the plans are complete, please brief us all."

Sitting at the office conference table, Douglas lifted a cut-glass tumbler and sipped the cool water before proceeding. "Cole, we have learned from the commander that Aludra has been taken to a terrorist training camp here in America, so we now have two objectives. The first is to neutralize the camp and the second is to safely deliver Aludra back to her sister in New York City. It is a small camp with eleven terrorist trainees and four experienced ISIS trainers, as best we can ascertain."

Clint asked, "Where is the ISIS training camp?"

"It would appear that ISIS has found a way into Canada and then across the U.S. border, going south to Missoula, Montana. The camp is west of Missoula in the Lolo National Forest. It is a parcel of several thousand square miles, making it easy to remain undetected. They likely feel at home in the mountainous region. We have an approximate location only. You and Meceli will handle this part of the operation. Speed is important, but we may have a little more time after Cole takes down the cells."

Clint thought through the possibilities and asked, "Do we know if they have satellite phone communication?"

"Unconfirmed at this point. That is why I said we *may* have more time. Ken's team has yet to break the satellite phone that Cole found in the commander's apartment. The camp leadership reports weekly with the ISIS commander by cell phone, so we can assume that is done when someone comes to town for basic supplies."

"One more thing; I would like to lead the takedown on the New York cell, Cole. Are you okay with that?"

Cole had a pensive face and puckered his lips in thought before replying, "I assume you want to make sure Amatullah is safe. Okay…and reassure her that she will not be charged under the circumstances."

Cole then turned to the director and asked, "Prisoners?"

"No, take them all down. You as well, Clint and Meceli. We need to send a very clear message that it isn't healthy to join ISIS and that ISIS can't operate successfully in America. The intelligence we need we are getting from the commander. Now, let's get to work. I will update the president. He will be very pleased that the nationwide address planned for Friday evening will be an announcement that the ISIS cells have been neutralized."

CHAPTER EIGHT:
THURSDAY

The success of the multiple city synchronized takedowns of all cell team members had three critical aspects; reconnaissance, location knowledge, and logistics—getting the team together in one place at the same time.

Cole had selected teams he had deployed for the cartel drug ring takedown some months ago. They had performed flawlessly then and he expected they would again. Logistically, he had arranged military transport to Kansas City, Costa Mesa, and Boise, and they were already on the ground. The team assigned to D.C. had already been hard at work.

His team leaders were in the process of acquiring building blueprints, doing eyes-on reconnaissance and scoping out any security measures that would need to be neutralized. Each of the six special ops team members that comprised each team had their assignments and would report by noon.

Cole used the ISIS commander's cell phone to text the cell leaders individually. The text simply said that he would be calling sometime in the early morning and would address the entire team and everyone needed to be in the cell's headquarters, no exceptions. That should ensure that the entire cell would be together for the takedown.

Clint would lead the NYC takedown, and Cole would oversee all operations from his D.C. command center where Russ was supervising all surveillance activities.

Meceli had been determined to find where the ISIS training camp was located in the Lolo National Forest. The area was massive and she requisitioned infrared satellite imagery in hopes of locating bodies, fires, lights—anything with a heat signature that would be out of place in the dense forest.

The imagery highlighted several options; hikers, campers, even clusters of animals—likely deer, bear, or mountain sheep. There was only one area that fit her qualifications and she requisitioned high-resolution photographic images of that location and a one-mile radius around it. It was a remote mountain area south of Route 12 that bisected the Lolo National Forest and was northeast of the Nez Perce Clearwater Forest subsection.

She had chosen this particular option because it was easily fifty miles away from any hiking path or public campground. Therefore, rifle target and explosives practice would not be overheard. They had the privacy they needed to train their killers and assassins. Murderers.

The camp abutted a steep cliff and covered a lot of ground. There were four buildings, the largest of which was likely the trainees' bunkhouse. The smallest was likely where Aludra was kept next to what she determined was the leadership's quarters. The last building had what looked like a canvas awning attached to what was a likely cookhouse based on the chimney and several crude benches and tables.

To the west of the buildings there were several objects that appeared to be obstacles, with a worn path suggesting an obstacle course as well as a target range. No doubt about it - this was the ISIS training ground.

Clint had returned to New York City to lead the cell's takedown. Knowing that there were only three operatives, the other two most likely having similar experience as Tabari, he decided to take the cell on his own. His plan was simple, have Amatullah call the three and order them to the Terminal Warehouse at the appointed time and for them to come separately, so as to not arouse suspicion, where Clint would be waiting, alone.

There was no intelligence to be gained from any of the three, so it would be quick and painless for them, but not for Clint. Taking a life in this way always left a scar on the taker.

Clint would then call and update Amatullah while heading back to D.C. to strategize with Meceli.

Each of the teams had reported in to Cole. Clint's was the quickest report as he knew the HQ location and layout, and had the cooperation of the cell leader.

He took the report from Team D.C. personally. The headquarters was in a single-story converted Holiday Inn, now low-rent office spaces, in northern D.C. The security would be easily compromised as it consisted of infrared motion detectors and a magnetic contact breaker on the main door. The cell consisted of four terrorists, and they seemed to be occupying two connected rooms. They were located in the rear of the building where the only other tenant was located at the opposite corner. Team D.C. was in go mode.

Team Kansas City reported a small cell of three terrorists working out of a Travel Lodge motel near the Greyhound bus station. There was no security short of a chain lock on the door. Team Kansas City was in go mode.

Team Boise had small but important issues. They also had a small cell of four terrorists, but were located in a vacant farmhouse surrounded by what once was cornfields, but now were barren dirt fields. There was very little cover, so approaching the house would be challenging, but doable. The house had an old alarm system that was inoperative. It was the dog that worried them. They would need to get close enough to use a tranquillizer dart, also doable. Team Boise was in go mode.

Team Costa Mesa was facing the most challenges. A team of seven terrorists had taken residence in a house near the South Coast Plaza in a seedy location. Part of the house was burnt out—the garage and a small porch that attached the garage to the house. Several vehicles were parked in the driveway and front lawn, and there was constant activity at all hours. There was no security technology to be compromised, but the activity would need to be dealt with when the time to neutralize was given. Team Costa Mesa was in go mode.

All teams, with the exception of New York City, upon given the "go" from Cole would cut the buildings' power and activate cell phone jamming devices. Night-vision goggles would give them the added advantage as they neutralized the cells. A detail from the Collaborative would then dispose of the bodies where they would not be found, ever. Their disappearance would add terror to potential new ISIS recruits.

Cole was satisfied that his infiltration teams were ready and briefed the director, who then briefed the president and was given the go ahead. Five AM Eastern Daylight Time was selected as a compromise—later than desired on the east coast, earlier than desired on the west coast—but synchronized takedowns were critical to prevent a warning call from one cell to another.

CHAPTER NINE:
FRIDAY

Douglas slept a few hours at his home before awaking at 3:30 Friday morning. When the alarm had fulfilled its purpose, he'd accidently knocked it off the bedside table in a failed attempt not to wake his wife. As he showered, she made coffee and served him a breakfast of scrambled egg whites, oatmeal, toast, and freshly squeezed orange juice.

His protective detail was waiting in the dark early morning, as arranged. At 4:15, he walked from the front door with his briefcase in one hand, a travel mug of steaming black coffee in the other.

Cole and Meceli had slept in their office, perhaps rested would be more accurate as what sleep had come was fitful. Pre-mission questions had—as they always did with the best operatives—plagued their subconscious. Had they missed something? What risk of life had they not covered, recovered? Did the teams have everything they need? Could they have done more to ensure success?

Douglas walked into the Collaborative's operations center noting, happily, that it was as alive as Grand Central

Station at commuting time. He could smell the tension, energy, and heat radiating from the computers and large LCD displays. It energized him and filled him with pride. His team was hard at work keeping America safe.

"Good morning, Director," Meceli said in an energetic tone, although her voice couldn't hide the sleep-deprived rasp.

"Morning Meceli. Have you slept?"

"Cole and I stayed here last night to ready the takedowns. He is getting us both coffee. Ah, here he is…"

"Good morning, Director. Everything is good to go." Cole said while handing Meceli a steaming mug of coffee.

"Good to hear, Cole. Tell your teams to move at precisely 5 AM Eastern and keep me current. I will be in my office." He wanted to stay and be part of the excitement, but recognized it was their show now and he might actually be in their way, and could possibly slow them down at a critical moment. He knew they were the best at what they did and his motto was "Put the best in the right place and get out of their way."

A single transmit button on the console was programmed to connect him live with each team. Cole looked at the time, acknowledged 4:54 with a glance to Meceli, and pressed it now, "All teams, mission is a go, repeat, a go at 0500 hours Eastern. Report status."

Each team in a prearranged sequence reported status as "go".

He and Meceli both wanted reconfirmation from intelligence that all cell team members were actually in their HQ locations, and got it with Russ giving them a thumbs up. Now, the most difficult period for a desk-bound operative - the waiting, the not knowing, the sleepless night's questions and doubts revisiting their consciousness once again.

***

Clint had met Amatullah late on Thursday to get a key to the Terminal Warehouse door. He was now in their Terminal Warehouse fifth floor room and had acknowledged the "go" a minute earlier, when he heard the freight elevator rising from the street level.

He knew it was one of the three terrorists because he had told Amatullah to stand down, and she had agreed.

Therefore, it was one, two, or all three of the terrorists. Then he heard the freight door slamming open on this floor, footfalls from one person coming closer, and then a key clicking into the lock on the door. There was total darkness in the room because Clint had pulled the old-style glass screw-in fuse earlier.

Clint's pupils were fully dilated, having been in the dark for nearly an hour, but not the terrorist coming in from the lighted hallway. As the terrorist stepped in, Clint recognized him as Tabari. He pushed the fact that he was a kid in a young man's body out of his consciousness, remembering that he was a terrorist who had pledged to kill Americans.

As Tabari turned to the left and flicked the light switch, Clint whipped his right arm around his neck, with the neck in the "V" of his arm, and with his right arm levered by the left arm in a chokehold. Clint's powerful arms squeezed tighter until he heard and felt Tabari's neck break in a near-painless death.

Clint then dragged Tabari's body well past the hinged side of the door and out of sight and waited for the freight elevator to lower to street level, alerting him to the next terrorist's arrival. And no sooner had the body of Tabari been placed, then the elevator began its roundtrip.

Again he listened to the footfalls after the freight elevator protested its use. This time there were two terrorists, the last two in this cell, but Clint was prepared.

Again, he waited for the key in the door lock as his signal. When the door opened, instead of coming in, just a right hand appeared and groped for the light switch. Switching it on and off several times and muttering about the fuse, the door opened slowly all the way.

Clint had no option but to strike. His training reminded him that with two adversaries, the key was to make a lightning-fast strike to incapacitate one, and then immediately confront the other.

Clint spun out of the dark room into the hallway light with his right hand already in motion, hitting the first terrorist in the throat, just below the chin. It connected perfectly and might have actually killed him, and at the very least it would surely take him out of this fight. The terrorist collapsed hard to the floor, halfway across the lighted hallway.

The other terrorist had managed to retrieve a knife and was now banishing it in sweeping left-right motions at Clint. His eyes were wide with fear and his teeth were bared like a rabid wolf. By the description Amatullah provided, this must be Hakim, Clint thought.

Clint tested his theory in Arabic, "Hakim, you will die this morning right where you are standing."

"You can speak English with me. Ask for forgiveness before I spill your infidel guts," Hakim replied as he lunged, targeting Clint's chest. Clint parried, grabbed the knife arm, and brought his knee up as he forced the knife arm down in one swift motion to hear the sickening crack of the bone breaking and the knife spilling to the floor. Clint then placed his hands on either side of Hakim's head and violently twisted the head, hearing the sound of Hakim's neck breaking.

Clint dragged Hakim into the room and placed the body beside Tabari's, and went back into the hallway to check on Hanabali. He had no pulse, obviously having died of suffocation from a collapsed trachea, and Clint moved his body to where the others lay and then locked the door as he left.

A block away from the warehouse, a non-descript van waited with the engine on. Clint passed the passenger side and paused when the window lowered and said, "Here is the key. Three down, no mess." No mess meant there was no blood to clean and that made their recovery of the bodies significantly easier.

Clint then checked in with the Collaborative's operations center by secure cell phone, saying simply, "Team NYC complete, three packages, no mess."

Clint then headed back to D.C. He was the taker of three lives with face-to-face intimate contact, and it affected him deeply as it always had. He had learned, from years of experience, that the greater good was what mattered, the saving of innocent American lives, and he placed these memories there.

Cole and Meceli both whispered to one another, "One down, four to go." Then Cole updated Douglas.

Only minutes passed before Kansas City checked in with, "Team Kansas City complete, three packages, mess." Directly on the heels of Kansas City, Boise checked in, "Team Boise complete, four packages, no mess."

Cole checked in with Douglas again, "Three down with two to go."

Meceli had finished her coffee and the caffeine amplified her nervous energy. Cole seemed capable of consuming endless cups of coffee without noticeable side effects, unless you watched his eyes grow wider and more intense.

Both Cole and Meceli jumped when Costa Mesa checked in, "Team Costa Mesa complete, seven packages, very messy."

They had expected that Team D.C., being local, would have checked in earlier and the worry was becoming palpable. "Cole, should we check in with D.C.?" Meceli asked with concern in her tone.

Cole thought for a second, looked at his watch and noting it was 0513, and said, "Let's give them another five minutes. No, cancel that, patch into their secure comms."

Meceli immediately keyed into Team D.C.'s live communications and both placed on their headsets to listen in.

"...the room is empty, no targets here. Looks like it was cleaned out. Wait one...BOMB! BOMB! Get out! Get..."

Cole and Meceli snapped their heads toward each other, acknowledging the horror of what they had just heard. Bomb. That clearly means team casualties. It also meant that the Collaborative had been expected, but how? They had missed something, or the recon team had been seen.

The recon team was comprised of the best of the best. It was very unlikely that they were made. But, surely they had missed something, and it may have caused team casualties. The enormity of having missed something flooded their thoughts as they waited for the team leader to check in.

"Team D.C. Leader."

"Go."

"We had a welcome present. Two team members down, two injured. Exfiltration to HQ now."

CHAPTER TEN

The mood in Director Douglas's office was a blend of somber and anger. Douglas was pacing around the conference table where Clint, Cole, and Meceli were seated. They were all exhausted, physically and mentally, but determined to find what they had missed—missed, because they were all in agreement that the recon team could not have been detected.

"Cole, good work on four takedowns. Let's keep focused on D.C. What happened?" Douglas asked.

"Director, the op was proceeding as planned. Security was deactivated, the door breached with precision, but the targets were gone. The team was clearing the room when a bomb was visually detected. They learned later that it was time-activated C4 placed on gas cans, triggered by the open door with a fifteen-second delay. Two operatives were too far into the room to escape. The two that were injured were close enough to the door to jump to relative safety, and will recover. We missed something, but don't know what at this time."

Clint jumped in, "It could be that the cell had a contingency plan if the commander didn't check in, but intuition tells me that isn't what we missed. We took down the commander less than eighteen hours before the takedown, so it just doesn't fit."

The team all nodded in agreement, pensive in thought.

Douglas broke the silence in an angered voice, "Clint, you must take out the training camp pronto. Meceli has briefed us on the recon and the ops team is ready. This is a critically important operation, more critical now that the D.C. terrorists are loose. We cannot let a single terrorist escape that camp. We need to send a brutally clear message to ISIS and potential recruits that they cannot operate within the United States…and if they try, they die."

"Understood, Director."

"Cole, we have four bad guys on the loose in D.C. Find them—"

Clint interrupted, "Director, we have six bad guys. I just thought of what we missed—the two hooded guys that abducted Amatullah's sister, Aludra."

"Oh my God, of course!" Meceli screamed. "We were so focused on the cells…Aludra's abduction was clean and well organized. Professionals. Experienced, too experienced to be part of the NYC cell. Could be leadership. Damn!"

"Good catch, Clint. I have six bad guys to find, and fast. We have been monitoring cell phones of the four terrorists, and that will provide prior habits as a starting point. But the two that abducted Aludra are completely unknown. I will interrogate the commander for more intel," Cole said.

"Good. I will update President Covey and suggest that his airtime tonight focus on the cells we have taken out, but leave out the D.C. cell, Aludra, and the camp. Questions?"

There were none.

The director authorized his Learjet to transport Clint, Meceli, and their seven-operative team to Montana. Meceli briefed Clint and the special ops team while inflight, and then pulled a blanket and pillow from the overhead bin, reclined her seat, and fell into a much-needed deep sleep.

Clint and the operations team lead, TJ Roach, sat alone in the aircraft's rear seats getting acquainted. TJ was a former Navy SEAL, as was Clint, which gave them instant mutual credibility. TJ, like all SEALs, had heard about Clint's legendary missions in Afghanistan. Many of his missions were now included in standard SEAL training and for TJ, deploying with Clint was an honor.

Clint went into the details of the operation with TJ asking questions for clarification. "TJ, you have reviewed the satellite recon so you know we are facing an armed force, probably semi-trained, estimated to be a dozen or so, and an estimated four trainers. We must assume that the trainers are experienced ISIS operatives."

"Experienced?"

"This is an assumption, of course, but we believe they are from Syria, which would mean they have Guerrilla tactical experience with light arms and explosives. If we are correct in our assumptions, they will not go down easily."

TJ thought through the intel being shared. "Got it. We will be able to validate those assumptions with eyes-on recon. We have two snipers on the team, and the other four I trust to have my back in any situation. Whatever we find, we will be ready, Clint."

"I have no doubts, brother. Get some shuteye. We will deploy immediately upon landing."

Soon, the aircraft cabin became eerily quiet. Air washing over the fuselage, soft snoring, the distant music from someone's earbuds, and the incessant jet engine whine were the only sounds. Experienced operatives always ate when food was available and slept when rest could be enjoyed, all knowing they may not get a chance later.

***

Back in D.C., the President of the United States was seated behind his desk in the Oval Office reviewing his notes for the live broadcast scheduled to start in two minutes. Satisfied with the brief but very important address, he stood, retrieved his suit jacket that was slung on the back of his chair, and slipped it on.

The beehive of activity checking sound, video, and lighting slowed to a stop and the President was given a countdown: "Five, four, three, two…"

Good evening. I have very important and positive news to share with you all. Most of you have read about the terrorist action in New York City this past Sunday. Thankfully, no American, indeed no person, was killed or seriously hurt in that action.

ISIS claimed responsibility and made a demand that America withdraw from Syria and if we did not withdraw, Americans in multiple cities would be placed in harm's way. The United States has a rigid policy of not negotiating with terrorists.

I ordered the Collaborative, led by Director Douglas, to find and neutralize the terrorist cell in New York City and to locate other possible ISIS cells elsewhere in America, and neutralize them as well.

I am very pleased to tell you that the Collaborative has neutralized the New York City cell and found and neutralized three additional cells in Kansas City, Costa Mesa, and Boise. Every terrorist in those cells was killed, and no American lives were lost while neutralizing these cells.

We must all remember—ISIS wants to bring fear into the daily life of every American. They only win if you fall victim to their strategy. I encourage you all to be strong and report any unusual activity to the local authorities.

We are a country at war and that war is fought anywhere we find the enemy. The Collaborative, FBI, CIA, Homeland

Security, State Department, Border Control, Armed Forces, and other departments have done an outstanding job in keeping the enemy and war from our soil.

Please understand this is not a religious war. ISIS is a political cult masked by a perversion of Islam, and misleads its followers that infidels are their enemy. Islam is a religion espousing peace and love. Muslims are a caring, loving, and peaceful people. There are bad individuals in every nationality, race, and creed. The few that have perverted Islam, ISIS, are not only our enemy, but that of nearly eighty countries worldwide, Muslim and non-Muslim alike.

Please know, ISIS has failed here in the United States and will fail in Syria!

God bless the United States of America.

CHAPTER ELEVEN:
SATURDAY & SUNDAY

The flight was uneventful and landed Saturday morning, several minutes earlier than planned as a result of favorable tailwinds, at a small private airstrip south of Missoula near the town of Lolo, Montana. Meceli had arranged for three nondescript vans driven by local FBI agents to meet the aircraft and was pleased to see them waiting by a vacant hangar.

Lolo was enjoying a wonderful early summer, with sunny skies and temperatures in the low seventies. Rain had passed through the valley several days before, leaving the roads and forested areas relatively dry.

The vans carrying the team and their equipment motored west on Route 12 for about sixty miles before turning left on what appeared to be an old mining road, more like a dirt path, really. Once hidden from the main road, the vans stopped and the team secured their gear, taking one last inventory to assure that no vital piece was lost or damaged in travel.

Meceli noted the GPS coordinates and confirmed with the FBI agents and the team that this would be the rendezvous location should they become separated. The vans then returned to their base. Clint addressed the team.

"Men, I have reviewed your jackets. Meceli and TJ have chosen well and I am proud to be in the field with each of you. I have your backs, you have mine, and we have the team—brothers. Well, and sister," Clint said with a chuckle. "Meceli saved my life on our last deployment, so don't cross her!"

"Okay. We believe the ISIS training camp is about fifty miles due south of our location. We are facing what we believe to be about a dozen semi-trained operatives and four hardened ISIS trainers, probably Syrian. Just like the camps some of you have confronted in Afghanistan and Syria, there are enslaved women, definitely one, probably more. We want to bring them home safely. All ISIS terrorists are to be neutralized—taken out with extreme prejudice. We will recon the camp soon, after we positively confirm its location and refine our tactical plan. TJ is your operational lead. Meceli is in charge should I go down. Questions?"

"Clint, what type of armaments are we likely facing?" One of the snipers asked.

"Good question. Meceli has satellite recon that shows AKs and evidence of explosives, probably C4. We assume small arms and knives as well. There is no evidence of anything larger, but we will know post recon."

"Clint, are the trainees all male? ISIS sometimes recruits females." The same sniper asked.

"Unknown at this point. But, this is important—gender has no role in terrorism. A terrorist is a terrorist, and your orders are to shoot to kill. Period. You hesitate and you die. The enslaved women will likely be chained to their beds and out of the field of fire."

"TJ, anything to add?"

"Yes, you all have a satellite radio. Keep them powered off. They are for emergency use only, with the exception of Meceli and Clint. No smoking. The wind could carry the burning tobacco smell and alert our enemy. Remember, there are campers and hikers in the Lolo National Forest and we want to be completely undetected so we move quietly. Let's move out."

The team moved in full stealth mode with Clint in the lead. A gentle summer breeze whispered through the red cedars and white bark pines, allowing the morning sunlight to intermittently peek through like a strobe light. They were moving quickly, even though they were now well off the mining road and now making their own trail in the hope of avoiding hikers.

Clint was not using a GPS to guide the team. His Indian heritage, and sense of being at home in the deep forest, gave him a natural internal compass. He looked at the sun's position regularly as a guide. Meceli, walking directly behind him, was in awe at how he made no noise at all. When she closed her eyes, she could hear nothing in front of her. It was as if he wasn't there.

Clint lifted his right hand in a fist, forearm up, indicating for the team to halt. He then disappeared only to return several minutes later, telling Meceli that the team needed to cross an open area with a running stream, and they would do this two at a time to reduce their profile and risk of detection. He then told her to pass it down the line.

Clint and Meceli crossed the stream and secluded themselves on the south side, covering the remaining team members. About thirty minutes later, the team continued south undetected.

Meceli took a GPS reading and determined that they had traveled nineteen miles by noon and suggested they break for food and rest. Clint agreed, indicating there was a secluded spot about a mile ahead, near an outcrop by the hill to the west. Meceli wondered how he would have this knowledge.

Cole had some good news from Russ and the team monitoring the cell phones of the D.C. cell. One cell phone was still in use at the same location they had tracked it to before the failed takedown. The question he now needed an answer to was, was it another trap?

He determined that the location needed recon and ordered a team to check it out and report back immediately. Their orders were to eyes-on verify that it was the same terrorist and if so, follow him in hopes that he would meet with the others.

Cole's next action was to check in with Ken and the lab team to learn of the progress in breaking into the commander's satellite phone, and was pleased to learn that they had made lots of progress. But it would be at least a day, maybe two, before the code was broken.

Leaving the lab, Cole headed for the detention facility to interrogate the commander. He needed the password and encryption key to the satellite phone and the identities of the two hooded men that abducted Aludra. This was time-sensitive critical intelligence.

Clint navigated the easiest but longest route to the ISIS camp. His thoughts were to keep the team hidden from hikers and conserve energy. Taking the shortest route over rocky hills, some would call mountains, risked injuries as well as being seen in the open. A loose rock tumbling down is noisy and a turned ankle would limit mobility and speed.

As dusk approached, Clint spied a secluded area within spruce and fir trees near a mountain stream. There the team made camp for the night. He risked a small fire in a deep pit for coffee while the team feasted on MREs, refilled their canteens, and rolling out their bedding. Refreshed and ready for sleep, he watched each team member disassemble their weapons, checking the actions and cleaning before reassembling. Solid men, professionals.

The black of night turned a pleasant summer's day into a chilly evening, the best sleeping temperatures for special ops.

"Clint, based on our rate of travel and current coordinates, we should reach the camp by noon tomorrow," Meceli advised.

"Thanks Meceli. You will take point tomorrow. I will lay out the route for you."

"Where will you be?"

"I will be gone by 0300, looking for the best location for our camp and will meet you on the trail to guide you in. Move out at 0600, no later, okay?"

"Good plan. Be careful," Meceli said placing her hand on Clint's forearm tenderly.

Cole stood looking through the one-way mirror at the ISIS commander. He was handcuffed to the metal chair, now dressed in orange prisoner garb instead of his tailored suit, looking more somber than the last time he had occupied that seat. Cole pondered how to approach the interrogation and concluded he should follow Meceli's lead.

He entered the room and immediately started, "Everything you have said in this room has been recorded and will continue to be recorded. Do you understand?"

"Yes, I assumed that."

"Good. You remember our deal?"

"Yes, I was killed and my family was released."

"Will be released. They are still in solitary confinement until we verify the information you have provided. We are having some difficulty verifying that you have provided ALL of the information. And I mean ALL!" Cole said in a loud authoritative tone.

In an exasperated tone the prisoner replied, "I have been truthful with you."

"Perhaps truthful, we will verify those facts soon. But we know you have NOT provided COMPLETE information, and that voids our deal!"

"You can't do that! I have answered every question truthfully!"

"We shall see. Answer this question: Who abducted Aludra al-Atassi?"

The question was received in total surprise. His face transmitted his knowledge and fear of ISIS reprisal on his family. He tried to swallow but a dry mouth made it difficult.

In nearly a whisper he responded, "You never asked me that question."

"I have now. I want their names, locations, cell phone numbers, and their position in your chain of command. And I want these answers RIGHT NOW!"

The prisoner closed his eyes and breathed out deeply before saying, "Our deal is still in place?"

"Answers first. You have nothing to lose and your families safety to gain."

"I report to them. They are responsible for all America ISIS activity and report to ISIS Syria. I do not know their names or locations, and we communicate only via satellite phone. I do not know to whom they report in Syria."

"We found a satellite phone in your apartment. Is that the phone you use to communicate?"

"Yes."

"What is the password and encryption key to unlock that phone?"

"It is a long password and key."

Handing him a note pad and pen, Cole said, "Write it down and print very legibly, because if it doesn't unlock that phone the first time we enter those codes, our deal is off."

Having the notepad with the codes back in hand, Cole said, "Good. One last question, for now. Tell me about the training camp in Montana."

Clint was gone three hours before the team broke camp. No one was aware that he had left the camp, earning him a new name, The Ghost. The team was comprised of highly trained and field-experienced special ops professionals, and for Clint to disappear undetected brought him an even greater level of respect.

By sunrise, he had made it to the terrorist training camp and found a shaded shelf overlooking the camp, about a half mile away. Using high-magnification binoculars, he started a meticulous survey of the camp and its occupants as the camp came to life.

A small bell was rung once, causing the trainees to pour out of their hut, sprinting into a single-line formation and placing their AK-47s on the ground. One leader faced the group as they counted off their numbers. Then they spaced out and started morning calisthenics. In classic military style, they went through deep knee bends, back stretching, toe touching, and pushups before running, AKs in hand, around the rifle range. So far, Clint was impressed with the discipline and conditioning routine.

Smoke appeared from what Meceli had guessed was the mess shack as the trainees were running around the target range. He estimated the circumference to be about one mile and wondered how many laps were required. They were all dressed in white t-shirts and camo pants, with black military-style boots.

The range had twelve sets of targets, spaced from the firing positions at about twenty yards, fifty yards, and then one hundred yards. To the left was a long steep rock face, which was easily three thousand feet high, sheltering both sound and sight. Forward of the range was a densely wooded hill of red cedar, spruce and fir. To the rear of the four huts there was a similar hill with a small stream flowing downward toward the camp, and together with the rock face on which he was lying, it created a hidden valley.

Clint concluded that the location was selected well, very well, a testimonial to the experienced ISIS camp leadership. In that valley, they had everything needed to live and train in near-total seclusion.

He counted eleven trainees and four leaders and murmured quietly to himself, "So the leader was telling the truth." His next task was to locate firing and recon positions for his team. That done, he belly-crawled carefully from his perch and headed to meet his team.

Clint was waiting for the team about two miles from the terrorist camp. He had located a narrow box canyon surrounded by steep rock faces that would provide a secluded base for their operation. At 1100 hours, he greeted Meceli and without stopping, led them to the canyon. An hour later, they were all resting and eating power bars.

He gathered the team around a sandy patch of ground and started the situation report. "Our intelligence was accurate—good work, Meceli. There are eleven trainees and four leaders, all in good condition. There is military precision in the camp and that will help our timing for the takedown."

Clint began drawing the camp layout in the sand, using rocks for the location of the huts. Then pointing to the areas for the recon team, he added, "I want you all to have eyes-on knowledge of the camp. We will do that this afternoon.

The best approaches are here, here, and here," he said while pointing with his drawing stick.

"I think the best firing positions for snipers are here and here. That gives you full field of view with a range of about four hundred yards. The assault team will probably be best split into two groups, here and here."

"The women, assuming there is more than one, were not mobile, so we must assume they are secured in this hut," Clint added, pointing at the last hut.

"TJ, these are my recommendations and we can refine our assault plan after your team returns from recon. Good?"

"Thanks, Clint. Okay guys, recon in complete stealth. You cannot be seen. Take Clint's suggestions, but validate them. Remember, his recon was from a single elevated position one half mile distant. It may look different from your actual position. Lastly, use caution as there may be bobby traps. Questions?"

There were none.

"Okay, move out and report back by dusk, no later."

The password and encryption key allowed the satellite phone to come alive and the lab was dumping the call logs. The next step would be to track the location of each of the numbers called in the last fourteen days, and then monitor each satellite phone.

"Ken, the satellite phone numbers I am most interested in are these based on their lat/long location," Cole said to Dr. Ken Turner while tearing a piece of paper from his notepad. "Those are the guys that abducted Aludra in NYC. As soon as you have a positive location, ping me."

"You got it, Cole."

**

The sun was slowly swallowed by the western hills and the closed canyon where the team was camped fell into darkness prematurely. Clint had allowed a roaring smokeless fire, knowing they were completely sheltered from view.

Each of TJ's recon team had reported back before dusk as ordered and, aided by the fire light, were refining the assault plan.

Clint and Meceli sat on a fallen tree trunk well away from the fire, enjoying steaming rich black coffee and talking quietly. The early evening air abruptly turned brisk as the sun set and the blanket of stars promised another sunny warm day tomorrow.

"Clint, Meceli, I think we have a good assault plan. Let me run you through it," TJ said.

As they walked over, the team opened their ranks to give them a view of the diagram drawn in the sand.

"Okay. Clint, your suggestions for firing positions were dead on, with the exception of this one," TJ said as he pointed to the one forward and north of the rifle range.

"You couldn't see it from where you were surveying that camp, but the densely packed wild rose bushes make it near impossible for a stealth approach. So, we will move Sniper One thirty yards to the east where there is a clear field of view and several felled trees for cover. Sniper Two will be exactly where you had suggested, here. Both have laser-measured the distance at three hundred yards to where you indicated they fall in at 0600."

Clint closed his eyes and placed himself in the terrorist camp thinking about the field of fire, and was satisfied that there was no possibility for harmful crossfire, and no obstruction to the field of fire. He opened his eyes and nodded to TJ as a signal to continue.

"I will handle overwatch, monitor communications, and be prepared to assist where needed from this position.

We plan to open the ball at 0600 when the trainees fall out for PT. As soon as they have lined up, the snipers will start; number one starting on the left, two starting on the right. We expect each sniper will get a minimum of three, probably four. Eight down, four remaining."

Again Clint closed his eyes and was mentally back in the terrorist camp. At three hundred yards, he reasoned a sniper could get off two shots before the first report would reach the trainees, then some confusion for the third and possibly forth shot. Made sense.

Leaving the leader until last also made sense since he had no weapon handy. Clint opened his eyes and nodded to TJ.

"Two assault teams will enter here and here. Their priority is the three remaining leaders that should be seated in the mess. Once neutralized, they move in support of the snipers to take out those remaining alive on the range."

"Clint, you and Meceli will secure the women, who are in this hut," TJ said, as he pointed to the last and smaller stone.

Clint added, "TJ, when the camp is secure, search every hut and body for cell or satellite phones, computers, and documents, and get them to Meceli. Get whatever can help us learn about their recruiting techniques, locations, planning, and reporting. Good plan, guys…it's a go!"

Clint then retrieved his satellite phone and called Cole to provide an update, who after the call, updated the director.

Now, they all waited.

CHAPTER TWELVE:
MONDAY

"The President will see you now," his assistant said to Director Douglas.

An eight o'clock Monday morning meeting with the president was difficult to get, especially when your request was made just an hour earlier.

"Good morning, Douglas," the president said from the sitting area of the office. "What have you got, good news I hope?"

"Good morning, Mr. President. Yes, progress. Ken's team has broken the satellite phone with the intel Cole got from the commander, and is now tracking all previous calls. There were four numbers, two of which are in New York City, and we assume they are the guys that kidnaped Aludra. One is in Montana, positively geographically located in the terrorist training camp. The other is in Syria. We assume he is ISIS leadership."

"That is very good news, Douglas. What about the four D.C. terrorists?"

"A cell phone was left in one of the terrorist's apartments the night of the failed takedown. We have eyes-on surveillance waiting for him to reunite with the three others that we are able to track. Our team has orders to take them all as soon as they are together," Douglas responded as he helped himself to a mug of coffee from the president's refreshment table.

President Covey pondered the new information while sipping his coffee and waited for Douglas to return to the sofa. "What's happening in Montana?"

"The assault team is likely in action right now. They scheduled the hit at 0600 Mountain Time, but we won't have an update until the camp is secured and the women cared for. I expect to get a report in another hour and will keep you informed, sir."

"Okay, Douglas. I can see it in your face. What haven't you told me that is worrying you?"

Douglas sipped his coffee as a way to delay his response as he organized his thoughts. "The two ISIS guys in New York are the head guys for their American operations. They are disciplined and smart; kept their names, locations, and faces compartmentalized. They must know that the cells have been taken out, except D.C. My gut tells me they organized the welcome gift that took the lives of two of our operatives. My worry is Amatullah. She has been told to stand down and out of sight, but these guys must know where she lives…"

"I see. Can we get her into protective custody?"

"Sure we can. That's not the problem. The problem is doing it without them seeing us do it. We don't know who they are and if they see that she is alive before we take them out, the only solution to keep Amatullah and her sister, Aludra, safe is witness protection. They will surely finger her as the informant and want retribution."

President Covey said, "Seems like we need to ID and take these guys out, fast!"

"Working on that Mr. President. Ken is triangulating the satellite phone with an active cell phone. When the satellite phone is activated, he will search for active cell phones and then we will have them. The challenge is the satellite phone is powered down except when in use. So, we wait until it powers on."

"So, we wait, but not patiently," the president said.

Douglas continued, "Yes, we wait. Our other worry is the satellite phone number to the camp in Montana. If they have warned the camp, we just don't know. Clint's recon suggested that they had not, as there is no evidence of added security. It would appear that the leaders believe we have no idea that the camp even exists. That is very good for us."

"So, we continue to wait and pray."

Meceli had placed some dry sticks and fanned the coals from the prior evening into a small fire. She was soon finished with making coffee, and the aroma roused the team to life at 0330 hours.

Each team member sipped coffee while completing their weapons check. Meceli had completed hers while the coffee was coming to a boil. Clint was a ghost again. They were an intimidating group, dressed in khaki and green camouflage with black grease-painted faces.

TJ was making his rounds, talking one-on-one with each of his team. He offered some words of encouragement, and checked their ammo and overall readiness. The team was ready.

Clint stood near the fire, magically appearing from nowhere, and addressed the team in a soft voice, "Our mission is the most important each of you have ever faced. If ISIS gets a foothold here, life in America will change; it will be a life that Americans have never known. You—all of us—have the ability and the responsibility not just to stop ISIS, but to send a brutally clear message to Syria and to any potential recruits that a painful death awaits terrorists. God be with you."

Not a word was uttered after Clint addressed the team. Weapons in arms, they followed Clint and melted into the dark forest in complete silence.

Douglas left the president's Oval Office and headed directly to the Collaborative's operations center, where he saw Cole in an excited conversation with Russ Jacobs. He walked briskly over to learn what had made them so excited.

"What's happening, guys?"

"One satellite phone powered on, and we were able to triangulate two cell phones at that location in New York City. The call was placed to Syria. We should send a team immediately."

"I agree, Cole. Please, get it done…but surveillance only until we know they are both our bad guys. Have a backup team stand by in the immediate location. I would like to take these guys alive, if possible, but in no case let them escape. Dead or preferably alive. Clear?"

"Crystal," Cole said as he reached for the phone.

Looking at his watch and noting a time of 0535, TJ expected his team to be in place and spoke softly into his shoulder mic, "Status?"

In the predetermined order, each of the groups reported themselves as ready. TJ then responded, "Wait for my go."

Clint and Meceli left TJ's overwatch position, moving south and closer to the hut where the women were being imprisoned. Meceli watched Clint closely, stepping where he stepped, moving when he moved, panthers in the early gray morning. Clint motioned with his right hand that they had arrived at their location.

They were favored to have a clear day; no rain and little wind. The sun would be rising soon and the bell would ring.

They again checked their weapons and when satisfied, knelt down to wait. Clint looked over to Meceli who was already looking at him, and smiled. It had the desired impact and she relaxed a bit. They both recognized there was more in their eyes than could be communicated at the moment.

Clint, nearly a foot taller than Meceli, could see the empty target range through the spruce bows in the pre-dawn light, and he kept actively listening for the single ring of the bell that would ready the team.

Seconds passed like minutes, minutes like hours. Birds were coming to life and an orange glow began to highlight the eastern hills like an aura. A gentle breeze brought the scent of cedar and spruce alive, flooding Clint with memories of his Indian boyhood.

The bell shook him back to the present and he watched as the trainees made their way to the range, carrying their AKs. He tapped Meceli on the arm and stood, Meceli following his action. The sun had cleared the eastern peaks and now began washing over the range as if a window shade was being lifted.

He couldn't hear the trainees counting off, but assumed they were when his earpiece barked, "Go!"

Clint watched as two trainees on the right fell, and by the time his eyes swung to the left two more were already down. He then heard the reports from the snipers, and another trainee went down.

"Let's move," Clint whispered to Meceli. It would take them about ninety seconds to reach the women's hut. As they were moving, they heard more sniper fire and then sporadic AK fire in return.

The assault team was armed with HK MP7a1 submachine guns fitted with suppressors, so their fire would be very quiet, like spits. The two snipers were using an unsuppressed Mk 12 Mod 1 which was their weapon of choice for this yardage.

Clint spied two trainees firing their AKs into the forest where the snipers were located, but they were useless at that long range so there was no concern that the snipers would be hit. The snipers would know that as well. When he next had a view, he saw that all eleven trainees were down as was the leader.

Reaching the hut, Clint took the right, Meceli the left. He then kicked the shabby door open so hard it broke from the crude hinges. Activating the muzzle-mounted light, he then jumped in and swept the small interior, finger on the trigger, but found it empty of terrorists. There were no standing bodies.

Three rude cots were against the rear wall, separated from one another by a green blanket suspended from a wire. Each cot had a woman covered by a dirty, gray threadbare blanket. The room was rank and smelled of human waste and body odor. A small table on the opposite side of the room had what appeared to be a lantern, candle, syringe, and a bowl of white powder.

The women were lethargic and had difficulty lifting their heads to see what was happening. They were drugged, he concluded. He then turned to see a wide-eyed and frightened Meceli moving slowly into the hut. A terrorist had a pistol pressed into her right temple.

"Drop your weapon, NOW!" The terrorist commanded. "Drop it or she dies!"

He locked eyes with Meceli and silently communicated instructions.

"Alright, I am putting it down. Don't shoot." He then very slowly placed the assault rifle on the floor and kicked it away, and raised his hands slowly over and behind his head to signifying his surrender.

Meceli then, using her left hand to enforce her right, drove her right elbow into the terrorist's ribs with tremendous force while she ducked slightly as the gun went off, the bullet missing her head by millimeters, the discharge burning her hair and drawing blood from her ear.

Clint had reached behind his head where a knife was holstered, and in one fast and fluid motion withdrew the knife and threw. It penetrated the terrorist to the hilt just above the bridge of his nose and he dropped to the floor like a wet noodle. Less than a second had elapsed between the pistol shot and his body falling dead on to the floor.

Meceli took a breath and collected herself while patting down her burning hair. "That was too damn close!" Her ear drum took a beating and was ringing and echoing, but she would survive.

Clint went to Meceli and embraced her briefly but warmly, feeling her quivering but holding it together. He then retrieved his weapon and put a foot on the terrorist's head, removing his knife. Wiping the blood on his shirt, he sheathed his knife as he made his way to the women.

Meceli was already trying to rouse the woman she recognized as Aludra. The woman was in a drugged stupor, with her left wrist bound to the cot with a handcuff. She was naked under the filthy blanket.

"Clint, these women are not ambulatory. We will need helicopter support to take them to our medical facility. I'll give them some water while you see if the camp is secure."

Clint spoke in his shoulder mic, "Women secure but not ambulatory. Report please."

TJ responded, obviously out of breath, "Twelve down, three missing."

"Make that thirteen down, we had a surprise here. Send a team here to secure the women's hut and I will meet you at the mess hut."

Team One arrived at the hut moments later and secured the perimeter. Clint headed to the mess hut.

TJ was talking with Team Two when he arrived.

"Two missing?" Clint asked TJ.

"Yeah, they were not in their hut, not here. Gone. We have scoured the immediate area, nothing."

Clint went to the leaders' hut while he was thinking through the disappearance. He knew they were here. Could they have left last night on a supply run? No, he concluded. They would do that in daylight, not darkness. Could they be hiding? Did they run?

As he poked around the hut, he noticed scrapes on the flooring near the legs of a cot. Something triggered a distant memory and intuition told him to investigate. He pushed the cot aside and noticed loose planking underneath. Lifting the planks carefully, he discovered crude a tunnel.

Of course, he thought. In Afghanistan, the Taliban were master tunnel makers. Damn! They would be a few miles away by now. The tunnel headed south, deeper into the Lolo National Forest. A plan immediately formed in his mind as he walked back to the mess hut.

"TJ, we have two runners. They escaped through a tunnel in the leaders' hut, heading south. My guess is they are a few miles away by now. Secure the electronics and documents, call in helicopters with medical support to evac the women and the team. Place all the bodies in the mess hut and fire it. Wait until the fire is out, then you evac. I will go after the runners."

"Clint, I will go with you."

"Thanks TJ, but with no disrespect, you would slow me down. I'm Indian and the forest is my home. Give Cole the situation report. I'll go and brief Meceli."

"One more thing, clear the tunnel please. I doubt the two runners are there but let's leave nothing to chance."

With that said, Clint turned and headed to the women's hut knowing that Meceli would protest. It would be easier to just head out but he couldn't do that, becoming more aware of his growing affection for her.

Meceli was cradling Aludra's head, trying to get her to take some fluids, when he entered. "Anne-Marie, we have two runners. They escaped through a tunnel in the leaders' hut. TJ is requesting helicopters to evac the women and medical assistance. Do what you can until they arrive. I am going after the runners, alone."

Clint continued, "When you have Aludra and the two others secured in the medical facility, contact Amatullah and arrange for her to be with her sister. I think it would be best to bring them to the D.C. headquarters."

She simply stared at him, aware that this was what he must do but fearful of the dangers. These were highly trained terrorists who had, no doubt, killed many times and would kill again…and they were born and raised in mountains similar to these. She gently lay Aludra's head down on the cot, rose, and came to him. She embraced him longingly and then, locking eyes, said, "You and I will enjoy dinner when you return. How does Italian sound?" she said, smiling affectionately, her eyes saying much more. Both remembering that was the same after-action plan in Peru.

Clint left the hut, turning back briefly and acknowledging Meceli's eyes with a smile, and went to talk with TJ. The team had dragged about half of the terrorists' bodies into the mess hut and the snipers had made their way back and helping to search the bodies and huts for electronics and documents.

"TJ, has the tunnel been cleared?"

"Cleared and, as you had expected, the runners are gone."

"How far did the tunnel go?"

"About fifty yards straight back. They probably used the tunnel making as a physical conditioning exercise for the trainees, and used the dirt to build small hills in their makeshift obstacle course."

"Now that we will have helicopter evac, better send a couple of men back to our camp to retrieve the packs. You should have time after you fire the mess hut. I will pick up mine and head after the runners. Anything else?"

"Yeah. I am ready to give the director the situation report. Is there anything you want me to pass on?"

"Yes, tell Cole that I will provide updates to him by satellite phone. My intuition tells me the runners are headed into the mountains south of us. They will be more comfortable there, knowing we are in pursuit. Make sure you have plenty of dry wood covering those bodies before you fire it. We want those bodies burned beyond recognition."

"Will do, Clint." TJ paused, then continued, "And Clint, you be careful. From what I have seen here, those two guys are experienced."

"Thank you, TJ. You did good work here. Let's try working with each other, and your team, again."

CHAPTER THIRTEEN

It was 0840 Mountain Time when Clint slipped the HK MP7a1 suppressed submachine gun over his shoulder and jogged back to the prior evening's camp to retrieve his pack. His mind was awash with calculations and questions.

He calculated that the runners would cover at least five miles of terrain every hour. Therefore, by the time he was back to the tunnel exit, it would be near 1030 hours and the runners would be over twenty miles distant.

He concluded that he must assume they had stashed provisions along the path as a contingency plan. They would also be armed, most likely with AK-47s.

That they would be running, he understood. It would, at the minimum, extend their lives and at best they would get away and be free again. He struggled, though, with how they would get away completely. Steal a car or camper from a hiking or vacationing family? Had they secreted some sort of transportation? If they did, what would their destination be?

Did they have Semtex or C4 explosives? Would they take revenge by initiating a terrorist action? All they really needed were the AKs to cause havoc.

All of these questions plagued his consciousness as he was jogging back to the tunnel exit. He determined that he must overtake them within forty-eight hours, maximum.

Nearing the approximate location of the tunnel exit, Clint slowed to a walk. His caution was fueled by his experience in Afghanistan where tunnels were often booby-trapped. Even though the tunnel itself was clear, it didn't mean the exit area was free of an unwelcome surprise.

Spying the exit, Clint began a slow and meticulous survey while hydrating himself. The exit was hidden between towering fir trees. The ground seemed undisturbed, but their experience would ensure it looked just like that. He ruled out a mine as during a quick evac one could easily stumble on it. Therefore, he looked for trigger wire.

Moving closer to the well-shaded exit, he ignited his rifle-mounted light and slowly panned the area looking for a reflection off the trigger wire. He saw it about six feet from the tunnel exit. He knew that he must disarm the bomb to prevent a hiker or animal triggering it.

Having carefully moved to the trigger wire, he noted that it was suspended about three inches high by a small rock on either side. He began carefully brushing the fir needles and leaves from the left point of ground entry and found it secured into the ground by a wooden stake. The explosive, then, was on the other side.

He settled carefully on the right side and began brushing the fir needles and leaves away. Then he saw the explosive. Not C4, and not Semtex. It was a grenade with the trigger wire attached to the pin. It was easy to disarm by simply cutting the trigger wire so that the pin would not be pulled. He disarmed it and placed the grenade into his vest pocket.

His worry now increased, knowing they had grenades. If he exploded the grenade, the runners might think they had slowed or stopped pursuit. But, if he didn't, they might think the tunnel wasn't found at all. After deliberating, Clint decided to go the second route, hoping that the terrorists grew too confident in their escape.

He then continued to scan the area for other dangers and found none, but noted from the boot prints they were headed due south. Clint concluded that they were hastily escaping and had time for only one trap. But, now Clint had to be very careful in his pursuit, and time didn't allow for that.

Clint decided that his best chance to catch them would be to take a shorter route to where he expected them to be heading. He reasoned that it was a risk—a huge risk—but what options had he? A booby-trapped trail would slow him to the point he would not be able to overtake them. The alternate route to their expected destination gave him a chance, if he could find one.

Retrieving his Lolo National Forest map and kneeling, Clint began his strategy. He surmised that they would take the hiking trail through the mountains into the Bitterroot National Forest. Edging slightly to the east would bring him close to Route 93. The likely exit point was a small town names Sula.

It was then that he remembered that there were hikers on the mountain trail that the terrorist runners would stumble onto, and those hikers would be at extreme risk of retribution. His decision made, Clint turned and returned to the camp.

Cole was in the Collaborative's operations center talking with the team from New York on his secure phone. Russ sat in an adjacent console, overhearing one side of the discussion, when Cole moved the phone away from his head and turned to him, asking, "Russ, are the two suspects still together?"

"Yes, the two cell phones we triangulated with the active satellite phone are still together at the same coordinates sent to the eyes-on team in NYC. They have not moved."

Without responding to Russ, Cole again spoke into his phone, "It's a go. Take them down, preferably alive, but do not lose them. Clear?"

Not able to hear the response, but assuming it was affirmative, Russ heard the last word from Cole, "Go."

Cloe then turned to Russ, "Keep active surveillance, please."

Clint walked into the terrorist camp wide of the burning mess hut, but still felt the intense radiating heat and the nauseating smell of burning flesh. The women were being brought to one of the two helicopters that had landed moments before in the open rifle range area.

He recognized the helicopters as Bell UH-1Y Venoms, sometimes referred to as Super Hueys, that likely came from a local military base. They could handle six stretchers and would bring the women to the local airfield where the director's jet would be waiting to transport them to D.C. Meceli was supervising the evac.

TJ was surprised to see Clint and hurried over to get an update on the situation.

"Surprised to see you, Clint. What's happening?"

"The path from the tunnel was booby-trapped with a tripwire and this." Clint reached into his pocket and retrieved the grenade.

"Not a total surprise but where could they get grenades, I wonder?"

"Irrelevant right now. I won't be able to overtake them if I have to clear every inch of the mountain trail."

"What's your plan, Clint?"

"I will have the helicopter take me to a few miles behind them. I am worried that they may come across unsuspecting hikers and take revenge for what we have done here."

"Makes sense, Clint. They won't likely find a place to land in the mountains. Do you still remember how to fast-rope?'" Then he chuckled and said, "Let me take you over to the 'copter pilot."

They headed immediately to the helicopter that was close to take off with the three women and Meceli.

"Major Burns, this is Colonel Bear, commander of this operation."

Burns extended his hand, "Pleased to meet you Colonel. I have heard of you, so when I say pleased, I really mean pleased!"

"The pleasure is mine, Major, and I need your help."

"Name it, sir!"

"I need you to drop me in the mountains immediately, right about here," Clint said as he retrieved his map and pointed to an area about twenty miles to the south.

The major studied the map for a moment and said, "We can do that. Fuel won't be a problem but I doubt we will find a place to land. You okay with a fast-rope deployment?"

"Not a problem, Major. Are you equipped with rope and gloves?"

"We have a rope in our kit, use it for training purposes. Don't know about gloves, though, so let me check."

Burns disappeared into the helicopter for a few moments before returning with leather utility gloves. "Colonel, most of the guys have their own gloves and keep them, but we have these. Try them on."

Clint looked at the gloves that resembled gardening gloves. Not ideal, but better than bare hands burning as he repelled downward. They fit, which surprised Clint as he had large hands. He then took another pair and, with difficulty, forced the second pair over the first.

"These will work, Major, thanks. I would like to get started right now if possible."

"Giddy-up, Colonel!"

He saw Meceli boarding the other helicopter, watching him, so and waved. She waved a tenuous, almost haunting, wave back.

Clint turned as he sat in the helicopter and yelled to TJ, "Better assign two men to clear the hiking path all the way through the Bitterroot, just in case."

"Good thinking, Clint. Will do. See you on the flip side!"

The NYC takedown team leader called the backup team with orders to take positions in the rear of the apartment building that was just south of West 14th Street on the Hudson Street. Team One would take the front and the takedown, while Team Two would watch and apprehend the terrorists should they escape through the rear.

The terrorist leaders were in the apartment on the second level with windows in both the front and rear. Team One was secreted in an alleyway off West 13th Street, which allowed them to approach the apartment without being seen from the windows.

"Team Two in position"

"Team One moving."

Breaching the locked entrance door to the apartment building was child's play, and the five team members made their way up the stairs, moving soundlessly to the apartment door. Two team members ducked below the door's peephole and took position on the left while two took position on the right.

The fifth member, carrying the battering ram, gripped the two handles tightly and looked to the leader. The leader flipped the stun grenade lever and gave the nod.

The battering ram hit the door with such force that it splintered the frame while sending the door wide open, slamming it against the inside wall. As the door opened, the leader threw the stun grenade into the room beyond the door. BOOM!

The explosion cracked the ceiling above them, plaster dust raining down on their helmets, and the two on the left poured into the room followed closely by the two on the right. The team immediately spread out, searching all areas of the apartment.

The room was well lit, with good visibility through the dust floating in the air from the stun grenade. One man, seated in an easy chair watching television, was stunned into unconsciousness. A team member went to him immediately, cleared a Glock from his lap, and zip tied his hands and feet.

To the left of the living room was an eat-in kitchen, and a pair of shoes was visible on the floor just outside the doorway. A team member went immediately to the shoes and found a young man lying unconscious on the floor beside a spilled plate of pasta. He had no weapons, and his hands and feet were quickly zip tied.

The rest of the team cleared the remaining three rooms: two bedrooms and a bathroom.

Through the earpieces a series of "Clear" was then heard by the team.

"Okay, check the apartment for electronics and documents."

The team leader then reported in to headquarters with a report. "Cole, apartment secured. Both alive and being evac'd to D.C. in a few moments, along with any electronics and documents found."

Clint was immediately taken back to Afghanistan as the helicopter took flight. How many times had he occupied this seat? How many operations had he led? How many soldiers had he and his teams saved? How many teammates were lost? Would this operation be successful...or would it be his last?

He had to stop those remembrances and focus on the here and now. The GPS coordinates he provided Burns would place him less than a half day behind the runners, if his calculations and assumptions were accurate. That would ensure the helicopter's engine noise would not be heard.

It was now nearing 1400 hours with plenty of daylight to work with. His plan was to use that time to move close enough to take the two terrorists the next day.

Minutes passed before Burns signaled that they were nearing the coordinates, and he was looking for the best place for Clint's safe deployment. They were hovering as low as they safely could, some one hundred and fifty feet above the ground. Thermals from the mountains were causing the helicopter to tilt, yaw, and bobble up and down.

Burns then turned the controls over to his co-pilot and came to assist Clint. "This looks to be the best place," he said as he double-checked the rope's anchor before throwing it out the open hatch.

"Good luck, Colonel!" Burns yelled to be heard over the engine noise.

With double gloves on, and his full pack secured on his back with his rife attached to the pack, paralleling his shoulders, Clint placed his right foot on the rail outside the helicopter while holding the rope. He wrapped the rope once around his left leg, leaving it draped over his left boot. He then stepped out entirely, pinching the rope between his boots and began his rapid decent.

As he sped downward, he felt the rope burning through the outer gloves and began to burn his hands, so he relaxed his grip a bit and increased his speed in the hopes of saving the gloves for a final pinch to slow the ultimate impact. Heat radiated through his left boot toe from the rope's friction, but he continued the pressure.

At what he judged as fifteen feet above ground, he tightened his grip to slow his decent. Just then, a thermal caused the helicopter to increase altitude. He was now closer to twenty-five feet, hands burning as the inside gloves began to fail. The helicopter decreased its altitude abruptly, and Clint released his hands and fell the last eight feet, landing hard but safely. He gave Burns an "all okay" wave as the rope was pulled back into the helicopter.

Burns then took the helicopter away at a low altitude to prevent detection as Clint marked his time and location. Clint then moved out, heading west toward the hiking trail.

Cole was sitting with Director Douglas at the conference table as he began the situation report.

"Sir, we have good news all around."

"Happy to hear that, Cole. What do you have for me?"

"First, the camp has been neutralized. All trainees are down, two of the leaders as well. There are three women en route to our facilities here in D.C. who were held in the camp, including Aludra. Meceli is escorting them with the medical team. All three were in heavy heroin-induced stupors."

"Cole, you said two leaders, correct?"

"Yes, sir. Two others escaped through a tunnel from the leaders' hut. Clint is in pursuit."

"I pity those two when Clint catches them. Correct that, I don't pity them one damn bit!"

"Agreed, Director. They are headed into the Bitterroot Forest. Clint expects to take them out tomorrow. The bodies and camp huts have been fired as you instructed."

"Good work Cole. How did the takedown go in New York?"

"We had a clean takedown and both men are in the interrogation facility. One surprise—it was father and son. The other leader is MIA. As soon as I can break the leader and get his satellite phone encryption codes, we will be able to start surveillance."

"Let's get to it. When Clint takes out the two runners and we find the last leader, we will have eliminated ISIS in America. The president will be very much relieved, and so will we. Good work, Cole!"

That history surrounded him was not lost on Clint. Old Bear had schooled Clint on the many American tribes over the years. He was remembering, as he scaled the Bitterroot Mountains, that back in 1805, the Corps of Discovery—led by Meriwether Lewis and William Clark, and aided by Sacajawea of the Shoshone Native American tribe—crossed the Bitterroot Range several times. Lewis first crossed the mountains at Lemhi Pass on August 12, then returned across the pass to meet Clark.

The entire expedition then crossed the pass to the Salmon River valley, and the next month entered the Bitterroot Valley from the south via either Lost Trail Pass or Chief Joseph Pass. It then crossed Lolo Pass to the west. The mountains were crossed by the Chicago, Milwaukee, St. Paul and Pacific Railroad, often just referred to as the "Milwaukee Road".

The Lakota Sioux had traveled these paths when they fled to Canada to escape persecution by the U.S. Army. And here, on these very same Indian paths, Clint, an American Indian, a Mandan raised Apache and a U.S. Covert Counterterrorism Operative, was in pursuit of two terrorists from a country that his Indian ancestors had never even heard of.

The sun was intense with a blanket of blue sky above, cloudless and still. The air was crisp and chilly at what he estimated to be an altitude of over seven thousand feet. It would be cold at night, he thought, something to consider for the takedown.

The path, when he found it, was on the west face of the Bitterroot Range. At a distance further west, he could make out the Nez Perce National Forest about forty miles away. There was still a good four hours or more of daylight and he must make good use of that time to close the gap.

Clint wished he had his moccasins instead of his military boots, to enable him to feel the earth and sense its teachings, but that was not to be and the boots would be warmer after sundown.

He established a cadence of scanning the path ahead for ten feet then gauging each foot placement for booby traps. The path was hard packed from weather—snow and rain— as well as deer and mountain sheep.

A small rock or stick displaced, a scuffed patch of moss, or loose earth was all cause for caution. All caused delays but could save his life and he was the only thing preventing a significant terrorist action.

The mountain trail was a snake, coiled with switchbacks as it wound around the face of the range. At times there was a view of perhaps a mile but no evidence of life. He needed to move more quickly to close the gap.

CHAPTER FOURTEEN

Cole sat pensively in the room next to the interrogation room where the American ISIS leader was restrained on the metal chair, pondering how he was to break this guy. He needed to know three things, and quickly. He could use the technique that Meceli had used, leveraging the cell leader's daughters and wife, but a son was different than daughters.

Rubbing his chin while looking at the restrained ISIS leader on the monitor, Cole tried to gauge his expression. What was he thinking? Was he fearful? Spiteful? Angry? Worried about his son?

The ISIS American leader sat erect and unmoving, eyes trained on the wall, unblinking, apparently calm and in control…or wanting them to believe so. His black hair neatly brushed and beard trimmed, he looked more like a businessman than a terrorist leader. He was a man that was accustomed to issuing orders and being feared; it was the power his status gave him.

Cole decided that he must break his feelings of status and prestige first, and then he would crumble. He rose and picked up the telephone, issuing orders to the listener. Replacing the telephone handset in its cradle, he then walked to the interrogation room while buttoning his suit jacket.

Cole watched the leader as he entered the interrogation room. There was no indication of surprise on his face, and his only movement was his eyes that met Cole's with a blend of disinterest and hatred.

"You are a terrorist and a prisoner of war. You have no rights. No one knows where you are, not even you. As a low-level functionary for ISIS, you have little information with which to bargain."

This brought a smirk to his face, showing his perfect white teeth contrasting with his black beard. But no words were uttered.

"Your son is in the same situation. He is an adult and will be treated as you will be treated."

The terrorist's head turned to face Cole, the smirk remaining, and he said, "And, how am I to be treated?"

Cole thought, Good, he is talking. "Since you will never see the light of day again, you will be treated as well as ISIS treats imprisoned Americans," Cole responded conversationally.

With a chuckle, the leader responded, "You and I both know that you can't do that. It is against your ridiculous American laws."

"Perhaps, but who is to know what happens in this room? No one knows that you and your son are here, do they? And…I am simply asked for information. I am not asked how I acquire that information."

No response. Good, Cole thought, he is processing his situation. A knock on the door interrupted the silence.

"Enter."

Two men and one woman entered. The men, formidable and dressed in dark suits, stationed themselves to the right and left of the door. The woman, wearing a white lab coat and safety glasses, entered last while pushing a cart, its wheels squeaking from lack of oil. The cart's top table was covered with a pale green sterile-like cloth, lumpy with whatever it covered. She maneuvered the cart close to the leader and removed the cloth. The leader, against his will, glanced at the implements on the cart.

Cole jumped in, "This is the wrong room; the son is in Interrogation Room Three."

"I am very sorry, Director," she said as she replaced the cloth covering the instruments and retraced her steps to the door.

Cole added, "I will be with you in a few moments. Please wait for me before you begin."

The leader was able—in that brief glance at the cart—to see that it contained several dental instruments: picks, drills, pliers, small hammers, and a tray of ice…and he realized the pain these simple tools could inflict. He also realized how the damage could be covered up with fillings.

Cole waited for the information to be processed before continuing.

"Now, where were we? Oh yes, as a man in your mid-level position, you have little information of value for us, especially now."

"Why do you say 'especially now'?"

"We have taken out all five of your cells. Oh, yes, and we have neutralized your training camp in Montana. They are all dead, bodies burned beyond recognition. ISIS has nothing left in America. You're through. You have failed yet again!"

Cole was using a tone rife with sarcasm, intending to inject humiliation into the terrorist's new reality to break any lingering feelings of importance he retained.

The leader's eyes closed and he inhaled a tentative breath, his once-erect shoulders now became rounded, slouched. Recognition that he had indeed failed visibly washed over his body.

"I will leave you now…unless you wish to talk. Your son is awaiting our newest interrogation technique. In truth, it is a bit old school, but they think it will be good to test it on the young."

The leader was turning his head subtly left and right as if motioning "no" before responding, "What do you wish to know?"

Clint chided himself. He needed to make up at least one full mile before darkness to have a chance to take down the runners in tomorrow's daylight. It was then he made a decision. Since there had been no booby traps for the last several miles even though there had been several ideal places to lay those traps, he concluded that the terrorists must believe they were safely away and not being followed.

He decided to double time the last of daylight and let his intuition guide him. It had always served him in the past and he believed Old Bear was with him now, guiding his intuition.

The mountain path was narrow with intermittent loose fallen rocks, uneven with patches of moss and lichen. One misstep and Clint could turn an ankle or break a limb…or worse, lose his balance and tumble off the ridge, plummeting hundreds of feet down to his death. Speed and accurate footing were both critical.

As he jogged down the path, a gentle cooling breeze brought hints of fir and western red cedar along with the dry taste of granite dust. Many miles to the west in the lower valley, he could see a lazy river flowing southward that he suspected was the Salmon River, but couldn't be sure.

His physical conditioning allowed him more than two hours of jogging without becoming winded, but as darkness fell he looked for a suitable secluded camp for the night. A small box canyon, more like an alcove no more than six feet around, proved the perfect place, secluded and shielded from the expectant night's cold breeze.

It was a dry and cold camp. A warming fire could not be risked. He feasted on power bars and an MRE, sipping water while watching the last of the orange rays of sun disappear under the western horizon.

Before sleeping, he navigated to a higher elevation to scope the range ahead. To his surprise, he saw not one but two fires. The first, a small fire, was about three miles ahead and the second, much larger fire, an additional two miles further away.

Worry flooded his being. He was certain that the small fire was in an earthen pit, a sign of experienced mountain men keeping a low profile. His runners. The second and larger fire was made with no thought or care of being seen. Hikers.

If he had seen their fire, the runners had as well and they were no doubt seeking revenge. It was only three miles to the runners, but in the dark he could not risk it. A turned ankle would mean the runners would escape. The sun would rise to the east and they were on the west side of the range, which would delay its impact on the trail.

Returning to his box canyon, he considered his options. There was no way to alert the hikers without also alerting the runners. And, even if he could alert the hikers, to what end? They don't know him and wouldn't believe they were in jeopardy.

Pulling his thermal blanket over his body as he lay facing the stars, he decided he must leave no later than 0400 and risk the mountain path in the moon's last dim light if he were to intercept the terrorist runners before they overtook the hikers.

Sleep was slow in coming, with his thoughts drifting to Meceli. Was she safe in D.C. with the three women? Was she thinking of him? The only sounds to distract his thoughts were from the slight breeze whistling through the range, the intermittent hooting of an owl, and the rhythmic beating of his heart. Eventually, sleep crept in.

Cole considered the leader's question as he took a step toward the door and reached for its handle. He turned and said, "I will give you one option, only one. Do you understand me?"

"Yes, I understand English."

"That is not what I asked you."

A sigh, "Yes, I understand."

"I will ask you three questions. One of which I know the answer. You will answer each of the questions completely, thoroughly, accurately. If you do not, your one option is gone. Forever. This is your one and only chance. Do you understand me?"

"Yes, I understand you. But what is this option you speak of?"

Cloe leaned over the chair, placing his hands on the chair arms covering the restraining handcuffs, his face within inches of the leader's face and replied, "Your son will be imprisoned, not interrogated with our new techniques. You will be treated in the same manner. I may even be able to arrange for you to be together. But one incomplete or inaccurate answer takes this off the table immediately and forever. Are you clear on this?"

"What guarantees do I have? Your word?" The smirk returned.

"Yes, my word."

Their eyes locked in mental battle, but Cole had all the advantage and the ISIS leader was well aware he had no alternative.

"I agree. You have given me your word and I have accepted it. What do you want to know?"

Cole pushed himself away from the chair and spoke very clearly, "Everything that is said in this room is recorded, so there is no possibility of an error in communication. So, the first question is this—where is your partner going, specifically, and how is he getting there?"

His shock that we were aware of the existence of his ISIS leadership partner in America could barely be contained. Eyes darting about the room was evidence he was searching for a way not to answer accurately, and Cole let him flirt with his desperation for only a moment longer.

"I asked you a question!"

The leader closed his eyes to the inevitability and then responded in a near whisper, "He is heading to Montana to meet the two training leaders that have escaped your attack. We were alerted to the attack shortly before you captured me."

"Very good, but you have only answered part of the question. Specifically, where is he going and how is he getting there? The next time you do not answer completely, I leave this room."

"He was planning to fly from LaGuardia airport through Chicago and on to Missoula, where he will rent a car to meet the two near Sula. I do not know the name he used to travel. They both have satellite phones and will coordinate the time and exact place to meet."

"Good. Now that wasn't so hard was it? Now, who do you report to specifically, and where is he located?"

"You will never find him so I don't worry about this question. His name is Abdul and that is the only name I have for him. He is in Syria and moves constantly."

"The last question is, what are your satellite phone encryption codes? Write them on this pad…"

***

Clint awoke at 0330, exactly as he had programmed his internal clock. Knowing this would be a long and difficult day, he gorged on more power bars and MREs, and hydrated thoroughly. He then repacked his equipment, cleaned his HK MP7a1 submachine gun and checked its suppressor, felt for his belt and back knives, and finally cleaned his handgun. He was ready.

His pupils were well dilated, and the half-moon in a cloudless sky provided better viewability than he had expected as he took to the trail.

The mountain trail at times narrowed to a mere six inches with a steep ledge to his left and a fall of hundreds of feet off to his right. Dark shadows from the nearly setting moon covered the path and he was forced to trust in his intuition.

Still, he was making excellent progress at a fast walk. Double time was out of the question until the sun rose.

An hour into his trek, Clint was brought to an abrupt halt. He nearly stepped over what appeared to be a hole but was actually twelve feet of emptiness—the path had washed away, and he nearly with it. There was no option but to scale the ledge upward and climb over the washed-out area. In the dark it could mean suicide, and the sun wouldn't rise for another hour or two.

Clint considered using the light beneath the suppressor on his machine gun, but discarded the thought as it might alert the runners. His only options were to wait until sunrise or attempt the climb. It distilled down to surviving the climb or putting the hikers' lives in the hands of the terrorists.

He started the climb.

The sun had risen an hour earlier, bringing life to Washington D.C. Meceli sat in the Collaborative's medical center, sipping coffee and awaiting the arrival of Amatullah. She was physically exhausted and mentally drained from supporting the three women during their travel from Montana.

The medical staff had started the women on methadone once they were in flight. They also started to hydrate them with IVs, adding antibiotics as a precaution just in case they had contracted a venereal disease.

She sipped from a paper cup of steaming black coffee as her thoughts drifted from the women to Clint. Where was he? Was he safe? Had he taken out the two escaped ISIS leaders?

Her thoughts were interrupted when Cole appeared, walking through the double doors and heading directly to where Meceli was seated.

"It is nice to see you, Meceli. You have done good work with these women, and I understand they will all make complete recoveries." He sat beside her and patted her hand affectionately.

"Thanks, Cole. Yes, they will make a complete physical recovery. But how will they deal with what they have been through, I just don't know. I can't even imagine."

"Their families will arrive in a few hours and they will hopefully give them the love and support these women will need to, in time, resume their lives. We have arranged for psychological therapy and we can't do any more. It will be up to them to move on. You have done more than anyone could ask, and that is a blessing."

"Thanks, Cole. Any word from Clint?"

"None. He said he would check in but I don't expect to hear from him until he has taken out the runners. My guess is that we'll hear from him by the end of day today. Don't worry, you will be the first person I update."

The sharp sound of heels on floor tiles caused both Cole and Meceli to look in the sound's direction. A tall, fashionably-dressed woman with long black hair and beautifully penetrating black eyes was briskly walking toward them with an escort. They both knew at once it was Amatullah, though she didn't match the description given to them by Clint as she was no longer dressed so conservatively and her hair was uncovered.

The escort introduced Agent Meceli, "Agent Meceli, I believe you were expecting Ms. Amatullah al-Atassi?" Amatullah stood anxiously with her "Escort Required" badge pinned to the lapel of her coat.

"Yes, thank you for escorting her here. I will take Amatullah to see her sister." Turning to Amatullah and extending her hand, Meceli said, "It is so very nice to meet you, Amatullah. Your sister is safe. Before we go in, may I introduce you to Cole Cunningham? He is the Director of Operations."

Cole extended his hand as well, "I am so happy we were able to recover your sister and keep her safe. Later, we will need to talk about how we can keep you both that way. But, now, go see your sister."

Amatullah was on the verge of being overcome with thankful emotion and replied, "Thank you both, words cannot do justice to my gratitude. And…where is Clint? Oh, please tell me he is safe!"

Meceli gently guided Amatullah by the arm while responding, "Yes, Amatullah, he is safe and should be back in a few days' time. Now, Aludra has been asking for you."

The cliff face ascended at nearly a seventy-degree angle— almost straight up. With such poor light, Clint had to squint to locate handholds—a crevasse, a small ledge, *anything* to help get across the washed-out portion of trail.

He spied what he hoped was a horizontal outcropping about eight feet above him and what looked like manmade handholds cut into the rock face to reach it. Without hesitating, he strapped the submachine gun over his left shoulder and started upward.

Clint's boots weren't ideal for climbing but they did provide good ankle support. He could only get a portion of the toe in the rock face's cuts, so his hands supported the majority of his weight. Four handholds later, he reached for the outcropping and was relieved to feel it was a six-inch protrusion.

He pulled himself up to where his chest rested against the outcropping, and struggled to find additional handholds to pull himself completely up and onto the outcropping. Here the rock face was moist, wetting his hands as he groped in the darkness.

Finding a handhold and securing his left hand fingers within it, he pulled himself upward. His wet fingers lost purchase and he began slipping downward. His submachine gun slipped off his shoulder and plummeted down hundreds of feet, well beyond retrieval. Struggling to stop the slide, his right hand found security on the ledge. Taking a breather, he dried his left hand on his pants and reached once again to the handhold.

Finally, secure on the ledge, he began to slowly slide his right foot over the ledge, never losing contact, reaching out with his right hand for the next handhold, and once secure, sliding his left foot to meet the right. This process continued until he could see the mountain trail below, at which time he pushed away from the rock face and plummeted the eight feet to the path.

Valuable time had been lost. A key weapon had been lost. The sun would rise in less than an hour and it would take longer than that to reach the runners' camp. He sipped his water and let his mind work through the problem.

How was he to save the hikers from danger? Without the submachine gun, he would need to be close. The runners were no doubt armed, likely with AKs, side arms, and knives. His priority was taking out the runners, but he could not let harm come to innocent Americans if there was a way to prevent it. In the end, he decided that plans would need to be improvised when he was closer to them.

Clint set off at a jog, risking all on the treacherous dimly lit mountain trail, with still more than three miles to reach the hikers' camp.

He let his mind travel at will and began to envision his people traveling the very path hundreds of years before. Circles. Then, they were escaping persecution, and he was now the persecutor.

CHAPTER FIFTEEN

Amatullah rushed through the door to Aludra's private room. She lay propped up in her hospital bed with plastic IV bags on her right side, tubes leading to her arm. A sterile alcohol-like fragrance permeated the room, but all that was lost on Amatullah as she hugged her sister.

Tears flowed freely from both women, as well as Meceli. She was happy that she had taken the time to have Aludra bathed and her hair brushed to lessen the shock on Amatullah.

"I will leave you alone now, but will wait outside if you need me. Take all the time you need. We have arranged a room for you to stay while Aludra is recovering."

Meceli left Aludra's room and quietly shut the door. She noticed Cole speaking animatedly on his cell phone, and waited for him to finish before asking, "News from Clint?"

"No, but good news all the same. Turner has unlocked the leader's satellite phone with the encryption codes and passed the information to Russ, who is setting up surveillance on ISIS leadership in Syria."

Meceli would have preferred it was Clint saying he was on the way back to D.C., but it was good news nonetheless.

***

The single benefit of losing the submachine gun was less weight and better balance. Clint was channeling the benefits to prevent getting overwhelmed by the liabilities.

The sun was rising and visibility improving, but he was still about a mile away from where he expected the hikers' camp to be, where the confrontation would certainly be.

Rounding a curve in the path, he stopped abruptly and moved very slowly back into the shadows. Clint was all too aware that the human eye was adept in seeing movement. Dropping his pack and retrieving his binoculars, he then belly-crawled out onto the path to view the area ahead.

Seconds passed until his worst fears became reality. The terrorists had caught the hikers where they had spent the night on a small plateau. There were four—two women and two men. The men were gagged and tied, both hands and feet, and propped up against the ledge. The women were tied to stakes, spread eagle and naked. Everyone was crying and all understood their helpless situation, as did Clint.

The terrorist leaders were drinking the hikers' coffee and eating their food, their AKs resting against the ledge nearby. They seem to be unaware and unconcerned about being followed.

Memories exploded in his mind of his fiancé Brook and sister Cabris having been violated by the cartel monsters before being brutally killed. His instant reaction was to kill and he had to control those instincts, not let the emotions control him. Years of training and experience allowed him to do just that.

Clint considered his options. Taking the path directly would get him to the plateau in less than ten minutes, but he couldn't do that without being seen. Going up and over the ridge would take an hour—too much time. He studied the path carefully and determined he could crawl a portion and run the portion that was concealed and, with luck, make it to a group of boulders that were no more than one hundred feet from the hikers' plateau.

He concluded that it was his only option to save the hikers, but it put his mission in jeopardy. If he was seen, he would be defenseless and the AKs had the range to take him out. He was determined not to be seen. Cutting some of the scrub and tucking it into the loops holes of his gun belt and leaving his pack, started the crawl.

As a boy, Old Bear had taught him how to blend with his environment. His camouflage coat and pants helped as well as the scrub he had fastened, but his ability to crawl like a snake, like an Indian, would make the difference.

Clint moved quickly but with complete stealth to the first secluded stretch where he could run. He was now close enough to hear their screams but dared not chance a look.

Reaching the next stretch of path where he could be seen, he dropped again and became a snake. Minutes passed, the screams growing louder as he neared the plateau. Less than two hundred feet to the boulders he had marked as his objective.

Sweat poured from his brow and stung his eyes, but he kept snaking to the boulders. Rock dust and dirt sprayed up and stuck to the sweat on his face.

The sun had begun to blanket the plateau, heating his back. A sharp rock caught his leg and tore through the camouflage pants and deeply into his thigh. He ignored the pain and continued snaking to the boulders. The rock dust, as fine as powdered sugar, caked his face and began blocking his nose. Still, he kept on.

He had done it! Resting against the boulders, he checked his side arm and knife and risked a peek around the side of the smallest rock. The two men were still gaged and tied. The two terrorists were standing in front of the women, unbuckling their pants. They would be hard pressed to reach their AKs. Now was the time.

Clint stood and walked out in plain view, less than one hundred feet away, pistol in his right hand. He offered no warning before he sighted and pulled the trigger, aiming for center mass. Four shots echoed through the range, two for each terrorist. All four shots were precisely placed and both terrorists fell back from the rounds' momentum.

One started to crawl toward the AKs and Clint fired again, and yet again. The women were still screaming, louder and more panicked than before, the horror of what was to happen and the unknown horror that they couldn't see fueling their terror.

Clint hurried to the men and cut their bindings while saying, "You are okay now. I am with the Collaborative and have been chasing these scum. Go see to your women. I will be right back."

With the men untied and comforting their women, Clint went to retrieve his pack. When he had returned, the women were clothed and sipping some coffee with shaking hands. They were all still in shock, but offered their thanks for saving their lives.

Clint said that he needed to report in and excused himself to get his satellite phone from the pack.

"Cole. It's Clint. The runners are down. They had taken four hikers as prisoners—two men and two women. They are all safe but badly shaken up."

"Glad to hear from you buddy, and happy you are safe. Meceli has been pestering me! Are the hiker's ambulatory?"

"Yeah, although I think they won't be hiking anytime soon, though. I will make my way back now."

"Sorry Clint, but there is one more to take out."

"Fill me in, Cole."

"We took out what we thought were the two American ISIS leaders, but it turned out it was one leader and his son. The other leader is en route to meet the two runners you just took down. During interrogation, we were told that he flew to Missoula where he was planning to rent a car and drive to the Sula area. Then he is to connect with them using a satellite phone."

Clint processed the new information. Sula was only about thirty miles due east. Had they already connected via satellite phone? Possibly. Was there a code phrase or sequence to validate each other? Possibly. Was there a predetermined time to connect? Possibly. All unknown to him.

"Cole, do you have any additional information? A description would be very helpful."

"Nothing Clint. But, Russ is working on surveillance, both cell and satellite phones."

"Cole, hold for a minute so I can search their packs for anything that might help."

Clint then went to the two small packs lying beside the two AKs and dumped the contents to the ground. The satellite phone was there as well as a cell phone, both powered off. Some dried food, water bottles, several grenades, and a map. Opening the map, he noticed an area west of Sula that was circled.

"Cole, the satellite phone is here but I would need the encryption codes to activate it. There is also a cell phone and a map with an area west of Sula circled."

"For now, that is your best bet. How long will it take you to get there?"

"Sula is about thirty miles due east, but I will need to summit the mountain to get there. Probably by late afternoon."

"Okay, call me when you get there and we may have a description and make of the vehicle from the rental agency in Missoula."

"Roger. Out."

Clint then turned his attention to the hikers, who seemed to be gathering themselves, making ready to move on. "Look, I know that you experienced a hell of a traumatic situation here. There are no more of these guys out here; these were the last two. So, you have nothing more to worry about if you intend to continue on your hike."

One of the women spoke first, "What is your name, sir?"

"Clint Bear, ma'am. Senior counterterrorism operative with the Collaborative."

"I...I should say we, can't thank you enough. If you hadn't come along when you did...I don't know what would have happened." Her voice was shaking and cracking, but coming on more normal as her adrenalin dissipated, and her tears had abated.

"I am just happy that there was no, well...happy I was able to get here in time."

She continued, "Who were these assholes?" She pointed at the two bleeding bodies.

Clint didn't want to answer truthfully, but realized that after what they had been through, they deserved to know the truth. "Ma'am, they were ISIS terrorists. The Collaborative neutralized their cells but these two escaped. Perhaps you heard about what happened in New York City last week?"

"Oh my God!" She sat pensively and put it all together. "They intended to kill us all!"

"Yes, ma'am. But, you are all right, all of you. I would like to note your names and addresses for my report, if you don't mind." He retrieved his notepad from his coat pocket and passed it to the man closest to him.

"If you don't mind me asking, what do you intend to do now? Continue your trek?"

They all looked at each other, hesitating, the doubt clear on their faces. They didn't know what to do.

"Let me offer this thought. You look to me like hiking is something you love to do. I have always found it best to face your fears and overcome them as quickly as possible. If you don't, you may run the risk of never hiking again. Are any of you experienced with firearms?"

"Yes, I did a tour in Afghanistan. Army." The smaller of the two men said.

"Good. Then you know the AK."

"Sure do. Lots of rounds fired at me from that weapon."

"If you want to continue your trek, you can take one of the AKs as added security. There are no more of these guys out here, so you won't need it, but it may make you feel more secure. Just drop it off at the nearest police station when you're back home, and give them my name if they have questions."

They all looked at each other and slowly began to nod. The woman said, "Thank you Clint, more than you can possibly know. We will continue, but it may take a while before we feel as safe as we once did."

Clint walked to the two AKs, picked one up and quickly disassembled the action, and checked it and the magazine. "It is fully functional with a full magazine." He said as he handed the weapon to the smaller man, muzzle up. "You should get moving so I can take care of the bodies and be on my way."

They swung their packs on and, as they headed to the trail, each went by Clint to shake his hand and say thank you once again. The women embraced him, their hugs seemingly saying, "Thank you for saving our lives."

Once they were on their way, Clint went through the dead terrorists' pockets but found nothing of value. Then he broke the stock of the remaining AK, disassembled the action completely, and threw the pieces in different directions. He took their belt knives and dragged them by the belt to the edge of the ridge. Looking down, he saw a deep crevasse several hundred feet below, and pushed both bodies to their final resting place. Food for insects and rodents—appropriate, he thought.

Cole had called Meceli to give her the news that Clint had taken out the runners but got her voicemail, and instead left a message suggesting she meet him in the operations center. He was talking with Russ, getting an update on the surveillance, when he saw Meceli quickly walking toward him.

"Cole, have you heard from Clint?"

"Sure have, Meceli. That is why I left you that voicemail. He reached the runners just as they had taken four hikers prisoner. It looked bad for them, but Clint was able to get to them before they were casualties. He took the runners both out and he is as healthy as the day you last saw him."

Tension melted from Meceli like an ice cube put to a flame, and the beautiful smile that had been missing over the last few days reappeared. It was very clear to Cole—and now to Russ—that Meceli had serious feelings for Clint.

Cole broke the silence that had become a bit awkward, "Russ, any surveillance updates for us?"

"Glad you asked. Yes, on two fronts. We have narrowed down the two satellite phone IDs to the last American ISIS leader and the head guy in Syria. The Syrian phone has remained, off but the American leader's phone goes on and off pretty regularly. We marked it in Missoula just a few minutes ago. The GPS coordinates place him at the regional airport."

"Good. Put a guy on the airport rental companies and find out the make and model of the vehicle he rented. Get a description as well."

Meceli quickly put things together, "Clint is to take him out?"

"Yes. He found a map in the runners' packs with an area near Sula circled. We assume that is the meet-up location. Assume…but we want to be certain."

Cole continued, "Russ, we need constant updates on that satellite phone location. Clint is making his way to the meet but won't get there until late today. The leader has only about eighty miles by car from Missoula to Sula. Clint has to go over the mountain to get there. Oh, and let me know the Syrian's location is as soon as he powers on the satellite phone."

Cole then left the operations center, heading to the director's office to update him in person. As he entered the elevator to take him up to the director's floor, he began to organize his thoughts.

While approaching the director's assistant's desk, he asked, "Is the director available?"

"Hello, Mr. Cunningham. He gave me instructions to give you access any time you need him, so go right in."

"Hello, Director. I have come with nothing but very good news."

"That is what I like to hear, Cole. Let me have it!"

"Clint has taken out the two runners, and just in time. They had taken four hikers prisoners, two men and two women. They were about to rape the women in front of the men when Clint took them out. They are shaken up, but otherwise fine."

"That's terrific news, Cole. Thank God!"

"It sure is. But there is more. Ken Turner has broken the American ISIS leader's satellite phone and now has active surveillance on both the last American ISIS leader's phone and the Syrian head honcho's. The last American leader in is a vehicle heading to Sula to meet the two runners."

Pausing, Cole let the director digest that information.

Is the plan to take the guy out?"

"Clint is heading to where we believe the meet is to take place. He found the location circled on a map when going through the dead runners' packs."

"Good work, Cole. Tell Russ as well. Now, any progress on the D.C. cell?"

"Status quo, Mr. Director. We have eyes on the one terrorist based on his cell phone and are waiting for the other three to join him...or for him to join them. The team has explicit orders to take them all down without collateral damage."

Cole was turning to leave the director's office, when the director asked him to stay a moment longer.

"Cole, I want a plan to take out the Syrian leader and any of his minions in close proximity. But I want to be absolutely confident that there will be no collateral damage."

Cole was only mildly surprised and responded, "We will get to work on it right away."

CHAPTER SIXTEEN

Clint sat leaning against the rock face and ate the last of his power bars, sipping his water while consulting the map. He would need to climb one last peak before working his way to a long, sloping valley as he headed to the Sula area.

He then inspected the cut on his thigh and concluded it needed a few stiches. Taking his medical kit from the pack, he removed the sterile suture vial. He cut away more of his pant leg to give him room to work and poured hydrogen peroxide over the wound, wincing from the sting. Wasting no time, he opened the suture vial and inserted the needle into his flesh, and began sewing. Tolerating the pain as he forced the needle through the cut and into the flesh on the other side, he repeated the process seven times. Satisfied that the sutures would hold, he slathered the wound in antibiotic ointment before covering it with a field bandage.

Throwing his pack over his shoulders, he started up the rock face. Favoring his leg just a bit at first, he learned quickly that he could move unencumbered while tolerating the pain, and began to climb faster.

Clint was able to move without the worry of being seen now that the runners were not a factor. He concluded he would make the summit by noon, perhaps sooner. Then it would be downhill, and once in the valley he could move much faster.

His mind was now at work on the last American ISIS leader. Was the circled location the meet? How would he be certain of his identity? How could he take him out?

Meceli suddenly flooded his thoughts. What was she doing now? Was she thinking of him now, as he was thinking of her? Her face, imprinted on his consciousness, was smiling radiantly. The sparkle in her radiant blue eyes warming his heart.

The climb was far easier than the last climb in the dark. Handholds and footholds were easily found, and the air, warmed by the sun but yet not yet in his face, made his effort less strenuous.

Reaching a small rock plateau near the peak after two hours of climbing, he paused to rest and hydrate. The air was noticeably thinner and colder, but not a hindrance to someone with Clint's physical stamina. He took a moment to appreciate the western vista. He could see for a hundred miles; snowcapped mountains and river-fed massive green valleys that were no doubt teeming with beaver, deer, bear, and mountain sheep, all unspoiled by man. It was as his ancestors had lived, and from it, Clint felt its connection in his soul.

Clint was fortunate to find a narrow game trail heading east and down after cresting the peak. The trail was part packed earth and stone dust, and part rock ledge, but it made his descent much faster and less strenuous. There was ample evidence of game dominated by mountain sheep and black bear.

He estimated that he would be a full two hours ahead of the original time he had provided to Cole, and decided to contact Cole when he made it to the base valley near the meet location.

***

Cole was walking into the operations center when he saw Russ waiving him over excitedly.

"What's up, Russ?"

"The team followed the D.C. runner to a self-storage facility in Virginia where he met with three others. They must be the ones we have been waiting for. We have tagged their cell phones and now have all four under surveillance."

Cole responded as he was heading to his console to contact the team leader, "Great news, Russ."

Meceli was already talking with the team leader, "Hold on, Cole is picking up."

"Cole here. What is the situation?"

"We have all four on visual at a self-storage facility. They opened the overhead door and entered, then closing the door behind them. We only had a limited view, but it looked like they had stored a lot of fire power in that unit."

"Are there any civilians near the unit?"

"Negative. Absolutely no other people around."

"Suggestions?"

"We fast approach with two on each side of the closed door. When the door reopens the first few inches, we throw in four grenades. That will take out all four for sure."

"Do it and report back!"

"Confirmed, operation is a go! Out."

Cole then sat at his console and briefed Meceli on the discussion with Director Douglas.

Meceli was processing the need for the Collaborative to take out the Syrian ISIS leader with the directive of no collateral damage. A drone strike would be the simplest way to take out a remote location, but that would not guarantee that there would be no collateral damage.

"Cole, I understand the director specifying no civilian casualties, but that will make the operation far more difficult to plan. Off the top of my head, the only way is to send in a team. What do you think?"

"You may be right. Let's start with satellite imagery of the location."

"Okay, I will get right on it and we can review it tomorrow morning. Is there a timeframe for this operation?"

"None stated, but the sooner the better."

"Let's connect to the team's comms; I would like to hear this live."

Pushing the console button, they both pulled their headphones on, sitting pensively as they listened.

"Team One in position on the right."
"Team Two in position on the left."
"The key is still in the door button so we can operate the door."
"Go, open the door a few inches and light 'em up!"
BOOM, BOOM, BOOM, BOOM!
"Targets all down."

"Team lead, this is Cole. We were listening. Report please."

"Cole, the door was blown off. Looks like the grenades took out all four runners and set off unknown ordnance in the storage unit. No team casualties."

"Good news. Secure the site please."

"Will do."

Meceli looked at Cole and said, "One more to go and then we focus on Syria."

Hours after the D.C. cell was finally neutralized, Clint made his way to the meet area west of Sula. Before contacting Cole, he decided to carefully recon the location.

The location was actually a picnic area with several stone fireplaces and picnic tables. A small paved parking lot abutted the grassy picnic area, with a single paved road leading in and out—to where he didn't know, but suspected it led to State Route 93.

The picnic area was man-made. Most trees had been removed, leaving very few places to secret himself. If the meet was at night it would be easy, but in broad daylight it would be difficult to get close enough to be confident in a pistol shot.

Clint sat thinking through the options. He had grenades taken from the runners' packs, and one under a vehicle would certainly take him out. He could pretend to be a camper cooking on one of the fireplaces to get closer to the parking lot, but that would risk being shot. He needed more time to think and decided to contact Cole.

Moving back to a concealed position, he fired up his satellite phone.

"Cole, I am in position."

"Good news, Clint. What does it look like?"

"It's a picnic area, wide open. Very difficult to get in close. No civilians at present."

"Hmmm. Not ideal. We have the vehicle. It is a Ford Explorer, white. Texas plates. The driver will be short of six feet, black hair and beard."

"That is something."

"What is your plan?"

"Don't know yet. Trying to work through the options."

"Okay. Be safe and contact me when you have taken him out."

Meceli had been busy redirecting a satellite to get the imagery they needed from the last coordinates of the Syrian satellite phone. Having sent the needed documents to the reconnaissance department, she sat and pondered Clint's situation.

And she prayed.

***

Clint had the best possible plan organized, and now put it into action. He began dragging dead branches to the small parking lot and placing them randomly into three of the four parking positions. He took care to make them look like they were blown into the parking lot at random. His hope was to guide the Ford Explorer into the one slot that was free of branches.

His next task was to dig a small hole in the center of the remaining parking slot. This was slow work as he needed to watch for approaching vehicles, and his only tool was his field knife.

Once the hole was dug, he placed one grenade in the hole and packed the loose asphalt around it to secure it in place.

Then he ran back to his pack and retrieved a nylon rope and began unbraiding it, making a thin but strong string, coiling it while he ran to one of the fireplaces. Clint then immersed the white nylon string in the cold ashes and rubbed the soot into the coil. Satisfied that the string would blend into the darkness, he ran back to the grenade. Then, he fastened the end to the grenade pin and carefully jogged back behind the closest fireplace.

Now he waited.

The last ISIS American leader might or might not come. Without the ability for him to communicate with the two runners, he could easily assume they had not made it and disappear. Or, this might not be the meet location. Only in time would he know.

Dusk would be upon him in about an hour, and still he waited. The temperature was falling, the breeze had ended, and the area was chillingly still. Birds were still active, with crows looking for food droppings near the trashcans.

In the distance he heard a slight rumbling and focusing his ears on it, detecting that it was moving closer. Soon he concluded it was a vehicle.

Minutes later, a white SUV came into view with the headlights on. It slowed as it approached the small parking area and then stopped at the entrance.

Clint could not see the occupant at this distance. What was the driver doing? Waiting for the runners to come out of hiding? Would he turn and leave if they didn't? Should he assume a runner's identity and show himself? No, he would wait.

Then slowly, the Ford Explorer moved further into the parking lot and toward the one available parking space. Finally, ever so cautiously, the Ford made its way into the parking space.

The shadow of a single head was visible—the driver. Cigarette smoke drifted out the open driver's side window. The Texas license plate attached to the front bumper seemed to radiate in the late afternoon's light.

Clint pulled the string…which pulled the pin from the grenade. Seconds later, the explosion lifted the Ford Explorer several feet into the air, igniting the fuel tank and instantly turning the vehicle into a fireball. The flames shot over one hundred feet skyward, and he could feel the heat even though he was nearly one hundred feet away.

No one in the vehicle could have survived.

All ISIS terrorists in America were down.

Powering on his satellite phone and securing a connection, he dialed. "Cole, the last terrorist is down. Please send a chopper to this location to pick me up."

"Will do, Clint. Stay put, I have your coordinates. The chopper team is on alert and should be there in less than twenty minutes. The director's plane is waiting for you at the airport. And Clint, we are working out a plan to take out the leader in Syria."

Clint watched as the hulk of metal that was once a Ford Explorer burned beyond recognition. The tires had exploded and now gave off thick, black, acrid smoke. The gas had burned off quickly and the interior plastics, rubber, and carpets were the source of the dwindling flames.

He heard the rotors in the distance before he saw the helicopter angling in for a landing. As soon as it touched down, he ran and jumped into the seat that he knew all too well.

"Hello, Colonel! Glad you made it."

Clint yelled to be heard over the engine, "Major Burns, thanks for the ride."

"Your chariot is fueled and waiting on the tarmac to take you to D.C. We will be there in about thirty minutes. Sit back and enjoy the ride. Sorry, no in-flight service," Major Burns screamed humorously as the helicopter lifted off.

The director's jet took to the air within minutes of Clint boarding. He helped himself to some sandwiches and bottled water, and settled into his seat for the five plus hour flight to D.C.

Refreshed and reclining in a very comfortable leather seat, his thoughts drifted back to the events over the past two days. But it was Meceli that dominated his mind; her striking blue eyes and the premature crow's feet that seemed to accentuate their intensity and softness; her lustrous chestnut-brown hair and the smile that radiated…then sleep overcame him.

CHAPTER SEVENTEEN: TUESDAY

Meceli was pouring over the satellite imagery of al-Raqqah, Syria, and then focused on the area south, past the Euphrates River, near the mountain range. The last satellite phone location was in the heart of the city, but she believed the Syrian leader would have a training camp in a more remote location.

Her thought process was logical; the location must provide secrecy, the ability to fire weapons without detection, and yet be close enough to al-Raqqah for the leader to live in comfort.

There were several potential locations that needed more detailed imagery, and she actioned the reconnaissance team with the locations.

Then, she left for the director's office for a situation report with Cole.

Meceli met Cole as he was entering the director's office.

"Morning, Meceli," Cole said cheerfully.

"Good morning, Cole."

Entering the office, the director said, "Get your beverage of choice and let's get to it." He was all business this morning.

After they were all seated at the conference table, the director said, "Cole, let's have the update. I will be briefing the president at ten."

As Cole was placing his mug of rich black coffee down on the table to start the report, the door opened and Clint walked in, looking like he had just returned from a Caribbean vacation.

"Well, this is a pleasant surprise! I didn't expect to see you until this afternoon, Clint," the director boomed as he rose to greet Clint. "You are looking well."

"Thanks, Director. I thought I would join you for the report."

Cole greeted Clint with a solid handshake and a slap on the back. Meceli waited at the table but beamed with excitement, seeing Clint healthy and home.

"Join us, please, and get a cup of coffee…you must need it," The director said as he and Cole seated themselves.

Cole started again, "Clint, brief us on the takedown in Sula and then we will address Syria. Okay with you, Director?"

The director nodded his approval.

"Well, not much more to what I reported before the takedown. I had lost my rifle while crossing a ledge, which required a close takedown. The environment prevented me from a secure stealth approach, so I needed to improvise by placing one of the runners' grenades in the pavement, tethered by a string to the pin. I placed loose branches over three of the four parking spaces, requiring the leader to park his Ford Explorer in the only available space. When I had positively ID'd the plates and he parked, I simply pulled the string. No collateral damage, no witnesses, and certain death."

Cole was impressed, as were Meceli and the director.

"Good work, Clint," the director said. "Now, let's move on to Syria. To bring you current, Clint, I want to take this Syrian leader out to prevent him from re-staffing his ISIS initiatives in America. And, I have insisted that there be no collateral damage. Cole, where are we?"

"Meceli has been pouring over several satellite images to locate where the ISIS team may be. We know the Syrian leader was in al-Raqqah, located in northern Syria and well south of the Turkey border. We are working under the theory that there is an ISIS training camp that is likely south of the Euphrates River, near the mountain ranges, that he supervises."

Cole paused to take a sip of coffee, allowing the team to process the information.

"We think the leader will want the comforts that the city affords, a common practice for someone of his rank. That is likely why we picked up his phone in the city. We are hoping to track his location, and perhaps his routine, by the satellite phone's GPS coordinates. Once we have the locations he frequents, we can determine the takedown strategy."

Clint sat quietly, as did Meceli beside him, processing the reconnaissance initiatives. Both were focused more on the "no collateral damage" objective.

The director said, "Timing?"

Cole let the question grow stale before replying carefully, "Difficult to determine. The satellite phone is only powered on sporadically. If our assumptions are correct, we expect the next coordinates to be the training camp. The first coordinates place him in the heart of al-Raqqah with a boatload of civilians around. The camp will likely be fortified with an unknown number of trained fighters."

Meceli added, "Taking out the camp with a drone attack should be plausible to prevent collateral damage, once we find it and positively determine the leader's presence. Taking him out within the city will likely require a surgical strike in the heart of bad-guy territory. But, another option is to take him out when en route to or from the city."

Clint jumped in, "All three are possible, but all have extreme risk to the assault team. My suggestion is to get the intelligence we need to select the best alternative. Director, what is your timing on this operation?"

Director Douglas sat pensively for a few moments before responding, "Obviously, the sooner we take him down the less time he has to rebuild ISIS here in America. But, I want this clean, very clean. Ideally, I would want him here in an interrogation cell. Before I brief the president, I want this completely buttoned up."

Clint probed further, "Director, why not use the assets on the ground—military or CIA?"

"Good question, Clint. It gets to the heart of why the Collaborative will head this operation. I can't be sure there are no leaks in either of those departments. I assume there aren't, but the number of people that would be exposed to the initiative substantially increases the risk of discovery by someone who shouldn't know that we have access to the leader's satellite phone. If he discovers that, we will have lost all connection with him, and I will not risk that. We will keep this compartment watertight. Understand?"

They all did and all were nodding their agreement.

"Good. Let's get to work and brief me when you have new data."

Cole, Clint, and Meceli walked together to the operations center to check in with Russ. He had the satellite phone device ID set up for automatic tracking that would log any other phones that were called, the geographic location by lat/long, the time and duration of the call, and would also record the call in its entirety.

His team had two Arabic-speaking specialists that were now tasked twelve hours on twelve hours off, seven days a week, to ensure there would be no delays transcribing the recordings.

Russ saw the threesome coming to his console and knew what their first question would be, and decided to answer it before being asked. "Hi guys. Nothing much new yet. The last geo location was the same as before, a residence in al-Raqqah. The call was made to a bank in Saudi Arabia to transfer $500,000 USD to a local bank. I have people looking into the accounts in both banks as I speak."

They were all aware that a terrorist operation needed hard cash for operations. One way al-Qaeda funded its operations was the sale of heroin, although affluent supporters played a significant role as well. Terrorists needed weapons, food, and clothing, but they also needed funds to bribe for access and favors.

Cole asked, "Russ, as soon as you have the owner of those accounts, the balances, and the recent activity worked out, let us all know. This could be a significant break."

"Will do, Cole. It shouldn't take more than twenty-four hours to break into their systems. If we are lucky, sooner than that."

Clint and Meceli went back to her console to look over the new satellite imagery. She had narrowed the focus to three areas south of the Euphrates River, just past Route 4 as it skirted the mountain range. Her thinking was that the Syrian leader would want ready access to his training camp from the comfort of his residence in al-Raqqah.

Clint spread out the black and white eight by ten photographs of what was marked *Area 1*.

Clint and Meceli searched the images intensely and wordlessly, each waiting for the other to complete their analysis. Meceli broke the silence.

"It looks like an abandoned manufacturing facility of some kind. The large building could hide the training facility, and there are several outbuildings that could be their quarters. But it looks completely abandoned. I see no signs of life."

"Agreed. Look at the approach, that single road into the main building. Grass has grown over the pavement. This place hasn't been used for several years."

While Clint was giving testimony to support Meceli's observations, she had replaced the photos with *Area 2*.

It only took a few minutes for them both to see that this one had potential.

Clint started the discussion, "It is odd to see what looks like a mosque in such a remote area, and there are several people milling about. I see evidence of lots of vehicles. Those smaller buildings could be used as quarters, a mess, and for support staff. The large open area would be adequate for training, especially with the few bombed-out buildings toward the rear. This area deserves much closer imaging. What do you think, Meceli?"

She nodded and focused on one photograph. Pointing to it, she said, "That looks like an antenna system. We need closer images, but my gut says it isn't a broadcast TV antenna. Looks more like short wave to me. Yup, closer imaging on this one."

After spreading out the *Area 3* images on the console table, they both immediately became disinterested. "This looks like a working sheep farm. The infrared signatures of the sheep are almost indistinguishable from a human. Good call, Meceli, but I think we should focus on number two."

"Agreed, Clint. I will order close-up imagery."

Clint paused, thinking, and Meceli knew the look and waited; she didn't want to interrupt his thoughts.

"Can you also get a drone into that location?"

"Sure."

"Let's do that and get a detailed video of Route 4 skirting the mountain range, and Route 6 going into al-Raqqah, especially the bridge over the Euphrates River. It will definitely help in our operation planning."

"Good thinking, Clint. I will take care of that. How about we get a cup of coffee and catch up? It isn't an Italian dinner, but for now it is the best I can do," she said while tenderly placing her hand on his left arm.

Cole decided it was time to visit Amatullah and her sister, Aludra. There was the issue of their safety to address, even though ISIS America was now a thing of the past.

As Cole entered the private hospital room in the Collaborative headquarters, he found Amatullah sitting bedside and saw Aludra's noticeably improved health. They were sitting and chatting, smiling and enjoying each other's company, confident in their safety.

"Hello, ladies. Sorry to intrude…"

Amatullah interrupted him, "No intrusion at all, Cole. We were hoping to see you today."

"Aludra, you look terrific! Feeling better?" Aludra looked to be a younger version of Amatullah. Her black eyes were soft, almost alluring, her tall slim frame accented by long black hair.

"Mr. Cunningham, I feel almost normal, physically. I can't explain how terrible it was in that camp, and how blessed I am that you and your team saved me and my sister."

"You are both more than welcome. And, call me Cole. Mr. Cunningham makes me feel as old!" Cole said with a short laugh. "I would like to give you an update and talk about your future. Okay?"

Amatullah replied, "Yes, please. That remains our biggest concern now."

Cole didn't want to breach security and the compartment that Director Douglas had insisted on, but after what these two women had done to help them and had been through, he decided to be truthful.

"This is for your ears only. Okay?"

Both Amatullah and Aludra nodded their agreement.

"Good. Based on the information and help that you provided, Amatullah, all ISIS operatives and leadership in America have been neutralized. The camp where you were held prisoner, Aludra, has been neutralized and all operatives killed. That includes the two leaders who escaped and were killed a day later by Clint."

They were both visibly relieved. "Bless you, Cole, Clint, Meceli, and the rest of your team. You have saved our lives and given us hope of having a normal life once again."

"Ladies, there is one loose end—the Syrian leader that planned the ISIS American operations. We don't know who he is, yet, but we know he is in al-Raqqah, Syria. And we intend to take him out as well. With him, well, out of the picture, all traces to you both will be gone."

"Al-Raqqah? I know that city. Our family visited friends that lived near the Euphrates when we were younger. Although now, the city has fallen into the hands of Al Qaeda and our friends left the city years ago."

"That is interesting, Amatullah. May I call on you for advice should we need it?"

"Cole, I will do anything to help you help America; just ask."

"Okay, thanks. Now, Aludra, the docs want to keep you for a few more days to make sure the effects of the heroin have been completely washed from your system. Is there anything you need?"

"Nothing, Cole. We have been treated like royalty. How will we ever repay you?"

"You already have. I will check in with you tomorrow."

CHAPTER EIGHTEEN: WEDNESDAY

The phone resting on Cole's bedside table vibrated, then vibrated again before he recognized it was an incoming call. As he sat up and reached for the phone, it vibrated off the table and smashed to the floor and vibrate-walked away from his grasp.

Finally, catching the rodent phone and pressing the button, he answered, "Cole."

"Cole. Russ. Sorry to wake you, but…"

"What time is it, Russ?"

"About four."

"This must be important, Russ. Go."

"The satellite phone powered on…remember, al-Raqqah is seven hours ahead of us. The lat/long is an area south of Route 4. And, there is more…"

"I will be there in approximately thirty minutes. Have coffee waiting."

Forty-six minutes later, Cole briskly walked into the Collaborative's operations center.

Russ handed Cole a mug of steaming black coffee and said, "You are going to be interested in this! I wouldn't have interrupted your much-needed beauty sleep if it wasn't important."

Cole, dressed in a pullover and chinos with a day's growth of beard, said, "I know, Russ. What do you have?"

"Okay, first; The Syrian leader's satellite phone powered on about ninety minutes ago. The lat/long places him right here," he said as he pointed to a map on his monitor. "That happens to be the location that Meceli and Clint thought was most promising location of the training camp, based on the satellite imagery."

"That is good news. We now have the likely location of the Syrian training camp."

"Yeah, but there is more, much more. We have broken into the bank's system. The account is owned by Farooq Abboud."

"That name rings a distant bell, but I can't place it."

"We did place it. He was the former Deputy Minister of Energy for Saudi Arabia. He was discharged after the king suspected fraud. It was rumored that he skimmed millions into his personal bank accounts."

"I remember that now. He was exiled from the Kingdom of Saudi Arabia seven or eight years ago."

"Yeah, that's the guy. The bank account in Saudi has a current balance of just over seven million USD. There is virtually nothing in the al-Raqqah account, which is no surprise. It isn't safe. But, the Saudi account is linked to a Swiss bank account, and although we haven't broken into that account, there have been transfers from the Saudi account to the Swiss account over the past ten years…of over ninety-five million dollars!"

"Holy shit! He could be financing the terrorist operations personally."

"Yeah."

"Good work, Russ. Tell your team as well. I need to update the director when he gets in. Keep up the surveillance."

"Will do, Cole."

"By the way, do you ever sleep?"

"I don't need beauty sleep," Russ replied while laughing.

Cole took what coffee was left to his console, dropped into the chair, and began to put the pieces together. He Googled "Farooq Abboud". What he learned both relieved and worried him.

Abboud was a brilliant man. Oxford-educated, majoring in finance and international law. The photo was ten years old and showed piercing black eyes, strong bearded chin, and a five-foot-eight well-muscled frame. It was the United States that had alerted the king that they suspected Abboud of fraud. He was known to be fanatical, since boyhood. He had served in the Saudi Special Forces after leaving the university. In short, he was smart, strategic, well trained, and a religious fanatic. Very, very dangerous.

Even though it was very early in the morning, he decided to visit with Amatullah, who had the room next to her sister's in the Collaborative's medical facility.

Cole entered the medical facility and went immediately to the night nurse.

Showing her his credentials, he asked, "I need to speak with Amatullah al-Atassi immediately. Will you please wake her?"

"Yes, sir. Right away."

Minutes later, the nurse left Amatullah's room and held the door open for Cole.

"Amatullah, I am sorry to have awakened you, but I need some help. May I ask you a few questions?"

"Yes, of course, Cole. Anything."

"Have you ever heard of a man named Farooq Abboud?"

"Oh my God, he is the Syrian leader of al-Qaeda! Oh yes, all Syrians know him, but most wish that they didn't."

Later that morning, the team met in the director's office for the daily situation report. Everyone was seated with coffee when Cole started in.

"Director, a great deal has happened in the past six hours. We have confirmed the location of the Syrian training camp by the leader's satellite phone's lat/long. It is the same area that Clint and Meceli thought was the most probable location."

The director said, "That's good news, Cole."

"We have also confirmed the identity of the Syrian leader. His name is Farooq Abboud…"

Clint broke in, "Abboud is a Saudi exiled from the Kingdom of Saudi Arabia for skimming cash."

"That's right, Clint. We've tracked ninety-five million of that skimmed cash to a Swiss bank account. He could be financing the terrorist operations himself. Mr. Director, I broke this compartment early this morning to get first-hand intelligence. I think you should hear it directly from the source."

The director was not pleased that Cole had disobeyed his direct order, but decided to let it go, for now. His policy of putting the right people in place and getting out of their way came instantly to mind. "Who have you added to the compartment, Cole?"

"I have asked her to join us here, and if you will allow me, I will show her in."

The director just nodded, sternly.

Cole rose from the table and went to the door. Opening it, Amatullah stood there, her nervousness evident. She was dressed very professionally in a fitted black skirt, white starched high-collar blouse, and a black vest. Her thick black hair hung below her shoulders, pulled back by a clip on the back of her head.

"Mr. Director, let me introduce you to Amatullah al-Atassi."

The director rose and greeted her professionally by offering his hand, which she shook gracefully.

"Amatullah, of course you know Clint and Meceli."

"Yes, of course, and it is very good to see Clint back and safe," she said as she sat at the conference table.

"Amatullah, I asked you this morning if you knew a man named Farooq Abboud. And you shared information that this team needs to hear. Would you mind?"

"Yes, I would be happy to tell you all that I know. Farooq Abboud is a monster; some think he is a psychopath, but all Syrians fear him. He is a religious fanatic with a perverted view of Islam. He kills at will and without remorse. He is the self-appointed Syrian leader of al-Qaeda."

Clint asked, "Al-Qaeda? Not ISIS?"

"Yes, Clint, al-Qaeda. You see, when Osama bin Laden was killed by your special forces, a void was left in their organization. Farooq filled that void but with a very different strategy. ISIS was then growing in awareness with their beheadings and press releases. It was Farooq that implemented a very different strategy from ISIS."

The director was beginning to see the logic in Cole's decision and asked, "What was the difference in his strategy?"

"It was brilliant, actually. Brutal but brilliant. He actually encouraged ISIS to the forefront because he knew that the free world would then focus on ISIS, thereby allowing him the time to quietly rebuild al-Qaeda into a stronger, more-connected organization. Eventually, the free world forces would eliminate ISIS and he would be fully ready to fill that void."

Meceli asked, "You stated a 'more-connected' organization. What does that mean, Amatullah?"

"Farooq has built alliances with similar terrorist groups, splinter groups, some local and some larger. The most important of which is Jabhat al-Nusra, based in Syria, with more than six thousand in their ranks at the last count. The common objective of the extended al-Qaeda organization is establishing a global caliphate."

Cole asked Amatullah, "Would you like tea?"

"Yes, please."

"Please, go on," the director said as Cole made her a cup of tea.

"Their strategy of lying in wait while the free world focuses on ISIS has allowed them to infiltrate all levels of government, establish a broad spectrum of relationships, and train a formidable army. They start with children, no older than fourteen to fifteen years old, both boys and girls. They have actually constructed a form of government with courts, social services, and control of the religious teachings in most mosques. To cross him means certain death to all family members. He is playing the long game, Director."

The director asked, "How is it you know all of this?"

"Mr. Director, even though I am a United States citizen now, I am a born Syrian and I have many friends with whom I correspond that still live in the most dangerous areas. My father was also once the president of Syria, and he ensured that his children learned about the political minefield surrounding us."

Clint put another piece together, "So, it wasn't ISIS here in America, but al-Qaeda posing as ISIS to further enrage America and increase our efforts to eliminate ISIS…giving al-Qaeda the ability to fill the void."

"Yes, Clint. That's it in a nutshell. As soon as Cole asked me about Farooq, it all fell into place for me. It also explained why they would put me in charge of a cell, the idea of which would be anathema to ISIS."

The director was unusually quiet, obviously thinking through the explosive information that Amatullah had provided. It was insightful and extremely well delivered. There could be no alternative motivation, other than to help the team before her and by extension the United States of America and the free Syrian people. He then made a decision.

"Amatullah, I understand that you have a Ph.D. in international law. Columbia, if I remember correctly?"

"Yes, that is correct, sir."

"I would like you to join the Collaborative, on my staff and part of this team, specializing in Middle Eastern analysis. Would you consider it?"

Amatullah was overwhelmed. This was completely unexpected. But, this would allow her the ability to help her adopted country as well as her homeland.

"Mr. Director, I would be honored. Yes, I can start right now!"

"You already have," the director replied. "I assume you will need your sister nearby, so we will find her a role in the business section when she recovers, if she is interested."

Amatullah was again brought to tears, but today, finally, they were happy tears.

"I will have the personnel department handle the appropriate paperwork. But, now, I would like you to work with Clint and Meceli. They have new imagery of the areas of most interest, and can benefit from your insight."

Clint, Meceli and Amatullah huddled at Meceli's console to begin the latest imagery review.

Meceli said, "I am very happy to have you on the team, Amatullah. Your experience and local knowledge will be invaluable as we begin to scope out this operation. Let's look at the drone video first."

Meceli then keyed the video to the large display and hit play. They watched in slow motion as the drone descended from the mountain range from the west. It was a soundless high-resolution black and white video that could be paused while zooming in on areas that warranted a more detailed look.

Amatullah caught on quickly and asked for Meceli to pause when a broad area with buildings came into view. "I know this place. It was once an enclave, like a small town or what the Israelis would call a kibbutz. There were a few hundred people here—livestock, sheep I think, homes, and a mosque. Can we zoom in?"

"Sure," Meceli said as she paused and zoomed in to reveal the action on the ground. Dozens of people were standing in twos, apparently facing one another, in the open area.

Clint put it in focus, "They are in hand-to-hand combat training. Zoom in more, Meceli."

They could now see that Clint was correct and that the people were young. Some looked no more than ten years old, both girls and boys. Amatullah's information was dead-on correct.

Clint then added, "It is clear that we can't take out this training camp. The press would eat us alive. Let's move on to Route 4."

Meceli then zoomed out and resumed the video at a higher speed until the drone began paralleling the route, and then slowed the video again. At the junction of Routes 4 and 6, she again paused the video and asked, "Amatullah, is the best way to the center of Ar Raqqah by Route 6?"

"To the center, yes. That would take you over the Euphrates. Route 6 bifurcates the city." The two-lane road was paved and in decent shape.

A plan was forming in Clint's mind. "Okay. Hear me out as I brainstorm. We can't take out Farooq at the camp for obvious reasons. We think that taking him out at his inner-city residence is very risky. The potential for innocent casualties is far too great. That suggests we look to take him out on the way to the camp or back to his residence from the camp."

Meceli was right with him, but this sort of thinking was very new to Amatullah, so she asked, "Why is his residence so risky?"

Clint, recognizing that she was new to this, paused to explain, "We believe his residence will be well fortified and well-guarded. It would require an operation similar to the one used to take out Osama bin Laden. But, being the inner city, getting in and out would be near impossible, not to mention the possibility of innocent Syrian casualties."

"I see; thank you."

Clint continued, "Okay, that leaves taking him out while traveling. The bridge can be our point. It is three to four miles from the camp, so if they heard gunfire or had a call for help and attempted a rescue, we would have at least ten if not fifteen minutes before they could respond. That gives us adequate time."

Meceli, as was her style, thought through his suggestion before responding, "I like the location, regardless of if he's coming to or going from his residence. Are you thinking the Euphrates?"

"I am. Getting into position will require helicopter support and we can't get to the bridge without a helicopter being seen. But, we could find a secluded area down or upriver where we could land and take CRRCs up the river."

Amatullah asked, "Sorry, what is a CRRC?"

"It is a Combat Rubber Raiding Craft used by the Navy SEALs. It is powered by an outboard motor and carries five to six people. We will need two CRCCs if we ultimately take this option."

Meceli added, "This approach makes a great deal of sense, Clint. But, we will need eyes-on the camp and the residence to know when he goes mobile. We can't rely on the satellite phone powering on. How will we accomplish that?"

They all recognized that as the vital piece in the high-level approach that they currently had no answer to, and Clint said, "Let's get Cole to poke holes in the approach and see if he has any ideas."

Cole joined the newly expanded team in a secure conference room located adjacent to the operations center. Clint, Meceli, and Amatullah were already seated when Cole entered the room.

"It's nice to see a new face on this team. I was getting tired of seeing your mugs!" he said with a chuckle.

"Okay, run me through the approach, Clint."

The high-resolution display had the drone video, as well as a Google Earth map of the area cued up and ready when needed.

Clint began, "The drone surveillance positively showed children in the training camp, so any strike there is off the table. We all agreed that a takedown at the residence, while possible, is highly risky. So, we focused on taking Farooq down when he is either en route to the camp or heading back from the camp to his residence. The best location for the takedown is here," he said, while pointing to the bridge over the Euphrates.

Clint paused to allow Cole to absorb the information before continuing.

"We would deploy well down or upriver in an isolated area. Helicopters in with CRCCs to the final destination.

The timing would be predicated on knowing when Farooq is mobile, and eyes-on will be needed. That is where we were hoping you could help, assuming you agree with the approach."

Cole walked over to the display and studied it for a few moments. He measured the distance from the camp to the bridge as well as the residence, and nodded.

"Have you picked a deploy location?"

"Not yet, but there are several options available if you approve the approach," Meceli replied.

Cole remained focused on the map and said while turning back to the group, "I like it, a lot. It provides a stealth approach and extraction, and limits the civilian involvement, especially if Farooq is mobile late in the evening. But, the timing could leave our team stranded downriver for hours or days. Do we have any mobile routines for Farooq?"

"Not yet, Cole. We have been limited to Farooq's use of the satellite phone. If we had his cell, it would be very helpful, but the lab has yet to ID it," Meceli replied. "It seems that if he has a cell, he keeps it powered off when using the satellite phone."

Amatullah spoke for the first time, "I may be able to help. Remember, I have friends and extended family in the area, and they all despise Farooq."

Cole questioned, "Would they be interested in helping us? This will be dangerous. We would be asking them to secret themselves near the residence and the training camp, and notify us when he is mobile."

Before Amatullah could respond, Clint amended Cole's statement, "I think the camp is the only location to monitor. They will see him arrive, providing clear intelligence that he is there. That will alert us to be ready.

Leaving the residence may not mean that the camp is his destination. In addition, he could stop at somewhere else along the way after leaving his residence, throwing our timing off."

"Good point, Clint."

Clint added, "This person needs to be a trained operator. We can't risk your friends, Amatullah. I am sorry, but I appreciate your suggestion. And, Cole, to work this plan effectively, I would like to bring in TJ Roach as he my choice for the operational leader."

Cole pondered Clint's suggestion and nodded in agreement. "Good thinking. Let me get the director's approval, but I don't expect there will be any issue. So, we will need to send in one of us in well before hand. Plan it out and be ready to brief the director in the morning. Good work!"

CHAPTER NINETEEN: THURSDAY

Cole got the director's approval to bring TJ Roach into the compartment, and by extension his team as the "boots on the ground" once the president gave the go-ahead.

The planning team now comprised of Clint, Meceli, Amatullah, and TJ. They were sequestered in a conference room working through the minute details of the takedown. In addition to the eyes-on needed at the camp, the additional challenges included their base of operations, where they would deploy, the location on the Euphrates where they would lie in wait, the operational deployment, weaponry, communications, and exfiltration.

The had made headway with the agreement that point of deployment would be the Mediterranean Sea from the USS *Dwight D. Eisenhower* Carrier Strike Group, which would maneuver to three hundred miles due west of their lie-in-wait location on the Euphrates.

Two choppers would be needed for the team, weapons, supplies and CRCCs. They would land about five miles west of the bridge in an uninhabited area, which would serve as their exfiltration point as well.

With that agreement, they next agreed that the best lie-in-wait position was an uninhabited island a little more than one mile west of the bridge, where there were adequate areas for concealment.

When they were alerted that Farooq was en route back to his residence, they would deploy and be in position within ten minutes. The snipers would position one hundred yards east and west of Route 6. Their job was to take out any escort vehicles. TJ would remain in the control role, monitoring communications. The four remaining special operations team members would be positioned east and west of the target location, spaced about twenty yards apart.

Clint had solved the eyes-on problem. He would make a HAHO—High Altitude – High Opening—parachute jump over the uninhabited mountain area south of the camp, the day before deployment. He would jump at thirty thousand feet to prevent ground personnel from detecting and worrying about what the aircraft was up to. He would make his way to a concealed position to monitor the camp entrance.

The team wasn't in full support of this tactic. They worried about how he would make it to safety after the takedown. It was Amatullah who provided the solution.

"If you can positively ID Farooq going into the camp, then it is just a matter of knowing when he leaves. We know he will not stay the night; he prefers the comfort of his residence. If you look topographically at Route 6, you'll see it is as flat as a pancake. Clint, you could walk the three to four miles in the hours Farooq is in the camp, and then use binoculars to monitor his leaving."

Clint liked the strategy immediately, "Terrific idea, Amatullah! That will also allow us more time to get in position."

Meceli then brought up the next subject. "The director has stated that the ideal outcome would be taking Farooq prisoner, but that taking him down is a mandatory minimum. Taking him down will not be difficult. Taking him prisoner may be a challenge."

"Good point, Meceli," TJ said. "Given his wealth, I expect him to be in a fortified vehicle and with support vehicles front and rear, minimally."

Amatullah added, "He was always seen in a black Mercedes sedan rumored to have bulletproof glass. I remember seeing pickup trucks in front and rear of his car, with machine guns mounted in the beds."

"Technicals," TJ added.

"Technicals?" Amatullah asked.

"Yeah, that's what we call fortified civilian vehicles," TJ explained. "The snipers will take them out as their first priority."

"We will lay spike strips to take out the forward vehicle and probably the Mercedes. The snipers may need to shoot the tires of the rear vehicle," TJ said.

Clint said, "Okay, we have the basic plan down, assuming we exfil on the CRCCs. You three work through the fine details and be ready for the president tomorrow morning. Nine AM sharp."

Clint went directly to the WET Room Department. The WET Room—Weapons, Explosives, Terrorism—was the brainchild of Dr. Charles Bommister, a brilliant and eccentric Naval Academy graduate. He was nicknamed Bom Bom by his classmates when an experiment in his dormitory room blew out the doors and windows.

Having gone through an additional two levels of security and finally through the thick, stainless steel door, he saw Dr. Bommister working on a mechanical device. He reminded Clint of Dr. Einstein in size, accent, and bushy gray hair.

Turning slightly, Bom Bom saw Clint approaching, "Hello Clint. This is a genuine and unexpected surprise!"

"Hello, Bom Bom. What crazy new device are you working on now?"

"I am happy to share this with you. But, before I do, I wish to congratulate you on your last mission. You accomplished what no one else could have in such a short time." Bom Bom was referring to the White Ice Peruvian cartel takedown.

"Thanks, Bom Bom. It was a team effort and you were a vital part of that success."

"Yes, well, I am working on a micro antitank mine. Micro because it is so small…and the magnesium projectile will burn clear through the largest and most fortified tank in existence."

"Impressive."

"You didn't come here to renew old acquaintances, though. How can I help?"

Clint detailed the mission while focusing on the problem areas. He needed a way to have eyes-on at a distance of four miles over at least three days, a way to stop three road vehicles at the same time, and a way to break through an armor-plated vehicle very quickly without harming the occupant.

"I see. The eyes-on is simple. Follow me, please." Bom Bom led Clint into a weapons stock room of sorts, containing virtually every weapon known to man. It was a massive room, more like a hangar.

"Lifting a small, stainless steel suitcase from a shelf, he said, "Here is your solution." He opened the case on a steel table and began assembling the contents. In minutes, he had a telescoping shaft attached to a tennis ball-shaped head.

"The shaft can be set to any height from one to six feet. The bubble, that is what we call it, is actually a high-resolution color camera and transmitter. You can remotely monitor it from this handheld device. The bubble has two axes of movement: right and left, up and down. The battery is actually located within the shaft and it lasts an average of seven days."

"That is perfect, Bom Bom!"

"Now, you need to stop three vehicles at the same time. Again, simple. Wait here and I will retrieve our PSS, Programmable Spike Strips." Bom Bom then walked to another aisle and retrieved three flat-coiled strips.

"Now, these are military-grade spike strips but are pressure activated. Notice this dial on the end?" Bom Bom said, as he pointed to a rotary dial at the end of the strip.

"The number zero through ten relate to the number of dual pressure pulses, front and rear tires, before it activates. So, set for two and after the second vehicle passes over the strip it will deploy and take out the tires of the third vehicle."

"Ingenious, Bom Bom. How would we ever make headway with this war on terrorism without you?"

"Your last challenge requires a two-step approach, but it is very fast because both steps can be accomplished in tandem." Bom Bom went to yet another aisle and retrieved another small, stainless steel case and a coil of what looked like pliable gray rope, sticky like putty.

He started his instructions as he opened the case, "This small puck is magnetic. Place it on the vehicle's roof and lift the lever on the top. This activates a titanium-tipped probe that will penetrate up to a full inch of armor and once through, releases a gas that will knock out all the occupants. They will be in fairy land for fifteen minutes. While the puck is doing its job, place this putty around the door frame and strike it once to activate it. It will burn a typical door frame off the hinges in less than sixty seconds. Voilà!"

Clint was impressed and very relieved. The possibility of taking Farooq alive had increased substantially. "You have made a huge impact on this mission's success, Bom Bom. I can't thank you enough!"

CHAPTER TWENTY:
FRIDAY

The team was already congregating in the White House Situation Room when Clint arrived. Meceli, Cole, and Amatullah were standing outside the closed door. The room was soundproofed, so they couldn't hear the discussion that the director, the president, and perhaps others were having, so they waited patiently.

The door opened a few minutes later, and the director invited the team into the room and made the introductions. Seated at the table, in addition to the president, were the Secretary of State, the Chairman of the Joint Chiefs, and the Attorney General.

The team quickly seated themselves and the director, taking the lead, asked Cole to outline the operation.

Cole went through the operation in detail, supported by maps and video surveillance, while the room otherwise remained silent. Everyone was aware that Syria was a designated war zone, so they were less concerned about territoriality and more concerned about team and civilian casualties. It was the president who broke the silence.

"Cole, what is your risk assessment?"

"We feel confident in the actual takedown. It is the time factor that increases the risk. The team will lie in wait on the uninhabited island for a minimum of a day and up to three days. They must be undetected. Less risk, but risk nonetheless, is the drop and exfiltration."

"Give it to me on a scale of one to ten, please."

"Four to six, Mr. President."

"If you are found on the island, what is your plan?"

"Immediate exfiltration upriver, sir."

"How does that impact Clint at the camp? He is some six miles away?"

"Yes, sir. He will make it by land to the exfiltration point and will need later transport."

The president looked at Clint and was greeted with a reassuring nod. "How will you handle civilian traffic on Route 6?"

"We are fortunate to have Amatullah al-Atassi on our team. She has firsthand knowledge of the area, and advises us that there is very little, if any, nighttime traffic on the road."

"Welcome, Ms. al-Atassi. And our sincere thank you for the help in ridding the ISIS America initiatives. You made a big contribution to the safety of the American people."

Amatullah blushed and replied, "You and my fellow Americans are quite welcome, Mr. President."

The Secretary of State, Elizabeth 'Liz' Madore, asked the next question, "How confident are you in capturing Farooq?"

Cole said, "Clint, would you address that question?"

"Sure. Using the president's scale, seven to eight. If we are unable to capture him, we will take him down, and that is a ten."

General Whitney Roads asked the next question, "You need support from the USS *Dwight D. Eisenhower* Carrier Strike Group. Two choppers and transport to the carrier from the States. I assume also a return is needed?"

Cole replied, "Yes, sir. If we are a go, we would like to deploy immediately. Can you make that happen, sir?"

"I see no problems there, Cole."

The president asked one last question, "Clint, how long has it been since your last HOHO jump?"

Clint had known this question was likely to be asked, and took a deep breath before responding. "It has been a while, but it is like riding a bicycle; you never forget. I am good to go."

The president looked around the Situation Room conference table, and seeing there were no remaining questions said, "Okay, the operation is go. Let's call it operation Mandan after a very good friend. My preference is to capture Farooq, bleed his finances to prevent others using them for nefarious purposes, and have him in extended interrogation. He could provide a wealth of al-Qaeda information. Come back in one piece—all of you!"

The USS *Dwight D. Eisenhower* Carrier Strike Group's configuration varies, but this tour was composed of roughly 7,500 personnel, an aircraft carrier, two cruisers, a flotilla of eight destroyers and two frigates, and a carrier air wing of seventy aircraft. A carrier strike group is the largest operational unit of the United States Navy, and comprises a principal element of U.S. power projection capability.

The Carrier Strike Group is a flexible naval force that can operate in confined waters or in the open ocean, during day and night, in all weather conditions. The principal role of the carrier and her air wing is to provide the primary offensive firepower, while the other ships provide defense and support. These roles are not exclusive, however. Other ships in the strike group sometimes undertake offensive operations like launching cruise missiles, and the carrier's air wing contributes to the strike group's defense through combat air patrols and airborne anti-submarine efforts. Therefore, from a command and control perspective, a carrier strike group is combat organized by mission rather than by platform.

The USS *Dwight D. Eisenhower* was the flagship for the Carrier Strike Group 10, commanded by Rear Admiral Keith Richards Lindsey. And his mission, as ordered by General Whitney Roads, was to support Clint Bear in every way he requested.

The entire team of Operation Mandan had landed on the deck of the USS *Dwight D. Eisenhower* just an hour ago, and were getting squared away in the visitors' quarters. Clint was the exception as he was getting prepared to deploy.

General Roads had pulled some strings and arranged for Clint to be flown to Muwaffaq Salti Air Base in Northeastern Jordan, where he would then board a Jordanian, but American made, C-17 transport for his HOHO jump over Syria. They had also agreed to allow a U.S. Navy Jumpmaster to deploy with Clint to provide a refresher on the jump techniques, as well as the new equipment he would be using.

Clint was due on the flight deck in thirty minutes and he wanted a final word with the team before he deployed. He entered the visitors' quarters and found the entire team lounging. They came into quiet focus on Clint.

Looking at each of the team he began his message, "I will deploy in a few minutes and won't see you again until we start the takedown. Farooq Abboud is a monster; that is how Amatullah described him. He kills at will, without remorse. He acts like he is the supreme ruler. He is enemy number one of the free world. He is financing the current and next generation of terrorists—kids, boys and girls."

He paused for effect, knowing the team needed to hear this to know their mission was of critical importance, before continuing, "We will stop the son of a bitch and slow the growth of terrorism in the region, and that just may give the free world the edge it needs to put a stop to their carnage…his carnage. We need to take him alive, sweat him, learn his secrets, and confiscate his money. And we will."

Clint was now going to share a modification to his strategy, "I have decided to take the timing initiative from him to us, by creating a diversion within the training camp that will require him to visit right away. If I am successful, the night you deploy, you will still head from the landing zone to the island, but be ready for immediate action. If we are lucky, you will proceed directly from the leave point to the bridge. This has not been approved because I did not ask. This stays with us. Meceli is the team lead. TJ is the operational lead. Let's go in and get out with our package. Operation Mandan is a go!"

Clint simply turned and left the room. Meceli did as well, following him. "Clint, that is a very dangerous change of plans, but I understand why you are doing it." She knew that the biggest danger was the team being spotted on the island and swarmed by Farooq's terrorists, and Clint's diversion would substantially decrease, hopefully eliminating that risk.

They stood facing each other on the gangway, eyes searching each other's, before they embraced. They both knew that this might be their last embrace and Meceli lifted her head, stepped on her tiptoes, and kissed Clint tenderly on the lips. Clint returned the kiss, withdrew, and then kissed Meceli again, longingly, before heading to the flight deck.

***

The Boeing C-17 Globemaster III was a large military transport aircraft, favored for High Altitude – High Open parachute jumps. The aircraft was developed for the United States Air Force in the 1980s by McDonnell Douglas and was powered by four Pratt & Whitney PW2000 jet engines. For its occupants, it was a noisy aircraft even from the beginning, but after thousands of flying hours it became nearly impossible to carry on a conversation without using a headset.

Jumpmaster Bob Fowler had volunteered for the assignment, partly because he was a SEAL and partly because he was unquestionably the most qualified. In the cargo bay, Clint was listening to every word Bob was saying through internal communications. They came through his headphones clearly, and he was well aware that what Bob was saying could save his life.

"Clint, this is all new equipment since you were active, but all the dangers are still the same. You remember the goggles that could freeze and break? Temperatures of thirty below freezing? Well, the new helmet prevents that and is connected to your O2 supply—that will take hypoxia out of the equation. You will jump at thirty thousand feet and fall at about forty feet per second until you pull the chute. If you black out, the new A2 will deploy your chute at the programmed altitude. I have set it for twenty thousand feet. Got it?"

"Copy that, Chief!"

"Now, you know it will be cold, damn cold, but the new jumpsuit will keep you at a cozy forty degrees. Every thousand feet you descend, you gain 3.6 degrees Fahrenheit in temperature. Piece of cake!"

Clint gave the jumpmaster a thumbs up.

"When you open the chute, there will be a physical shock. Now, you packed light but your weight combined with your pack and weapon will make that shock extreme. Its gonna feel like your legs are being ripped off, so be ready."

"Copy that!"

"Use your GPS regularly to stay on course. This chute will allow you to steer more effectively than the older ones that you were accustomed to."

Clint nodded.

"Okay. Let's take those headphones off and get the helmet on and locked. Then we can check the O2."

The jumpmaster picked up the helmet, placed it over Clint's head and secured it. Then he attached the O2 hose and turned the O2 valve, checked its pressure and looked to Clint. The O2 was drawn in from natural breathing, just like a scuba diver.

Clint gave a thumbs up, signaling the oxygen was flowing.

Clint was suited and ready, but Bob was busy triple checking all the equipment and when satisfied, patted Clint on both shoulders and gave him a thumbs up. It was near midnight.

The red two-minute warning light began to flash. The jumpmaster needed to leave the platform before the rear door lowered and depressurized the jump area. He gave Clint one more thumbs up, a pat on the helmet, and then rushed into the pressurized cabin.

Clint watched the rear platform door lower into blackness and then focused on the red blinking light waiting for the adjacent green light to flash—go. His thoughts drifted to Meceli and the green light flashed. Without hesitation he ran down the door, now a ramp, and jumped into total darkness.

Clint was immediately thrown by the C-17's wash but as he plummeted toward Syria and out of the turbulent jet's wash, he gained control. He watched his digital altimeter counting down the altitude and chills flowed over his body as he felt the cold seep into his jumpsuit.

He was traveling at forty feet per second, just under thirty miles per hour, and it would still take four minutes to reach his target of twenty thousand feet. Seconds passed like hours in the black of the night. Air was whispering past his helmet, the O2 hose vibrating in its turbulence as he headed toward earth helmet first.

As he reached twenty-five thousand feet, he adjusted his body position into a spread eagle—arms and legs out to slow his decent and thereby lessen the impact when he deployed the chute.

At twenty thousand feet, he let the chute fly and braced for the impact. It hit like he had jumped off a ten-story building and hit the ground, but without the broken bones and death. The impact was so powerful, he looked down to make sure his boots were still on, and they were.

Clint then powered on the GPS display and discovered he was nearly ten miles off course. But that wasn't a big concern as he had nearly twenty thousand feet and a very maneuverable parachute. He pulled the right hand-pull and began angling to the target mountain range.

He could see the lights of al-Raqqah in the far distance, but there were none anywhere near his target landing zone. The tricky part now was to land in a flat area to prevent breaking a leg or ankle. As he got closer, he spied the perfect location in the half-moon's light, and headed directly for it.

About ten feet from the landing zone, he pulled both hand-pulls to soften the impact, and it worked perfectly. He then pulled the chute fully down and began gathering it, and looked for a place to bury the chute and suit. Having done that, he began his trek down the mountain range to find the best place to observe the camp before the sun rose.

Clint's plan was to recon the training camp during the day. He found a suitable location about three hundred yards to the south in the mountain range, with a small ledge above him and several boulders in front. Securing his pack and pushing several small rocks out of the way, he sat to rest and await the morning light. It was chilly, but his thin thermal blanket would keep him warm. He downed some power bars and water and prepared for sleep, and it came quickly.

CHAPTER TWENTY-ONE: SATURDAY

Clint awoke as the sun was fighting through the heavy gray clouds. His selected position placed the sun to his right, which would prevent reflections off the lenses of his binoculars. As the day was breaking, he began his meticulous reconnaissance of the camp's interior.

With the binoculars pressed against his eyes, he smiled, knowing that Meceli would be awake as well and reviewing weather projections and triple checking their preparation for tonight's deployment.

The camp looked a bit different now, as it had the dimension that a photograph or video couldn't provide. The entire compound was walled with stone and concrete that he estimated to be eight to ten feet high. No razor wire topped the wall. Was it to keep people out or keep the trainees in, he wondered?

There was a covered sentry tower on the west side of the main gate that appeared to be manned with a heavy weapon, probably a machine gun of some type. No other towers were visible, and no roving guards. Good, he thought. They are not overly concerned with an attack.

All the buildings were located within the walls. A long metal-roofed building was located on the east side, probably the trainees' barracks. A large sprawling building, located on the north wall close to the main gate, was probably the leaders' domicile, as there were three technicals parked in front. A small shed that contained large barrels, probably fuel, stood alone near the west side of the gate with a latrine about thirty yards from the shed. The only other building within the compound was the mosque on the south side.

The open area in the middle of the compound was where the satellite photos had showed the hand-to-hand combat training within the rifle target range. A few trees towered over the wall and scrub dotted the walls' perimeter.

Clint, having seen what he needed for now, sat down and began to think through his diversion strategy.

He was focused on planning a diversion that could be implemented this evening, ideally just a few hours after dark. That would time it as Meceli's team was in the air heading to the landing zone. If he could time it perfectly, Farooq would be en route to the training camp as the team formed at the landing zone, just five miles up the Euphrates and only fifteen to twenty minutes from the bridge. That would obviate the need for a risky layover on the island.

The type of diversionary tactic was his first of many decisions. He concluded that an assault tactic of any type was out. That would raise concerns and Farooq might go underground for personal security. Therefore, he concluded, it must look accidental. That brought the shed and the fuel barrels into focus.

Retrieving his binoculars, Clint began a close examination of the shed and its contents. Definitely fuel, he concluded, and a hand pump was attached to one of the six barrels. He then examined the west wall and concluded that the trees would allow him a stealth approach, and would likely help him over the wall. His concern was that it was only thirty yards from the manned guard tower. He sat back down in thought.

As he was thinking through his tactical plan, he began hearing noise from the camp. The trainees were in the center of the compound doing morning calisthenics while the leaders floated within their ranks.

They were girls and boys; some could be as young as ten years old. Those that were not able to keep the leaders' desired pace were being struck with what looked like riding crops. The noises he had heard were the screams as a trainee was whipped into submission.

The worst of the leaders was a large muscular man, perhaps in his thirties, wearing a black knitted cap, a military camouflage combat vest, gray pants, with an AK strapped across his chest. He appeared to be in charge and was barking orders to both the trainees and other leaders.

He approached one emaciated boy that was struggling with pushups, and kicked him repeatedly in the chest before moving on to a girl that was on her knees, fighting for air. He offered her his hand as a gesture for her to stand. She stood on weak, shaking legs and the leader struck her in the face with a closed fist, delivering such force that she was lifted from her feet, landing roughly about four feet away. She remained motionless on her back.

The leader walked past the girl and spat on her.

Clint's adrenaline immediately pulsed through his body. He wanted to kill that bastard, slowly and painfully, while watching the life seep from his worthless body. It was clear that many of these children, perhaps all, were imprisoned as opposed to being volunteers, probably hostages with their families' lives at stake. The wall was to keep the trainees in, preventing an escape.

He couldn't watch this brutality any longer, and knowing that he would not sleep tonight, lay back to rest until dark.

Meceli was personally checking the equipment now loaded into two UH-60 Black Hawk helicopters on the flight deck of the USS *Dwight D. Eisenhower*. Satisfied, she headed to the operations center where the team was assembled.

TJ had his team fully prepared, and they went quiet as she entered the room. They were dressed in desert camouflage with black-streaked faces; all very intimidating and a force to be reckoned with.

"Men, the weather is working with us. We have no winds or rain forecast for the next three days. Therefore, we will use our planned approach. We will fly due east and have been cleared over Jordan. Once entering Syrian airspace, we will turn due north to the landing zone. We will be traveling at nineteen thousand feet over largely unpopulated areas until we near the landing zone."

She paused to catch a breath before continuing, "We will deploy immediately at the landing zone, ready the CRCCs, and wait for Clint's diversion…I expect that will take place shortly after we arrive. Our priority is to take Farooq alive, but failing that, take him out. The choppers will be grounded in a secluded area about thirty miles south of the landing zone, ready for a rapid evac. TJ is the operational lead. Questions?"

There were none. "TJ, anything to add?"

"Yes, thank you, Meceli. You all know your positions; we've been over that many times. I want to stress that the director wants no, make that zero, collateral damage. Farooq and his convoy are our only targets. By the way, you will all have two weeks R&R when we return, so be safe."

There was universal applause for the R&R as they made their way to the flight deck.

Darkness had settled over the compound and, with it, the constant brutality had ceased. The compound was quiet, with the only life evident in the guard tower and a periodic visit to the latrine.

Clint began his approach at 2000 hours by heading west and then north to approach the western wall undetected. The half-moon provided adequate light to secure the proper footing, but not enough to skyline himself. Good fortune, he thought.

He was about two hundred yards from the stand of trees that he intended to use to scale the wall behind the fuel shack. Using his binoculars, he checked the compound again and found it clear. Moving his view to the guard tower, he could see one guard, who was focused on the access road from the junction of Routes 4 and 6. Good, he thought, his back is toward me.

Reaching the trees and satisfied that he could scale the wall easily, he retrieved a rope from his pack and threw it over the wall, securing the other end to the largest tree trunk. Leaving his pack and assault rifle behind, but taking a timer and a small charge, he scaled the tree and reached the top of the wall. Grasping the rope, he slithered over the wall and soundlessly slid into the compound behind the fuel shack.

Once on the ground, he immediately scanned the compound grounds and saw the brutal leader walking toward the latrine some twenty yards to his right. Glancing briefly to the guard tower, he was relieved to see that the guard had not moved. He then altered his plan.

Clint moved without hesitation toward the latrine, staying close to the wall to prevent shadows. Standing next to the latrine he smelled cigarette smoke, which meant the leader was sitting with pants around his ankles. He quickly scanned the compound once again and, seeing no activity, he moved.

He pulled the door open, and in one swift movement hit the leader with a powerful throat crush, stifling any calls for help while quietly closing the latrine door. He looked into the leader's eyes, now wide in fear, and hit him repeatedly in the face until he was sure he was at best dead but at least unconscious. Clint then spat in the leader's bloody face, knowing he would not be brutalizing children ever again.

Opening the door a few inches and seeing the compound clear, he lifted the body on his shoulder in a fireman's carry and brought the leader over to the fuel shack. He then pulled the leader's pants up and began the diversion.

Very slowly and carefully, Clint pumped fuel from the active drum onto the ground around the other drums, until the entire area was puddled with gas. From his pocket he took the timer and small charge, and placed them on the bottom side of the drum. He set the charge for thirty minutes and dragged the leader's body close to the drum. He was satisfied that the diversion would look accidental at worst, and at best, it would look like the leader's doing. Either way, it would cause Farooq to visit, immediately.

Back over the wall, with the rope coiled in his pack, Clint then set out to place the camera.

Several hundred miles to the west, the two UH-60 Black Hawk choppers had just cleared into Jordan airspace. They were immediately met by two Jordanian fighters tasked to escort them safely through to the Syrian border.

Meceli and TJ were in separate choppers, just in case one were to go down due to a mechanical failure or attack.

The teams sat patiently, quieting their minds and resting their bodies as best they could. The choppers vibrated unmercifully, the engine and rotor blade noise preventing verbal communication. At nineteen thousand feet, they all were wearing oxygen masks anyway.

Clint consumed Meceli's thoughts. Was the HAHO jump successful? Was he safe? Had he devised a diversion plan? Would it work? Would she see him again...?

As the Black Hawks were being escorted safely through Jordanian airspace, Clint was moving west through a lightly forested expanse that was peppered with small and medium-sized rocks. He moved quickly from cover to cover, keeping his moonlit shadow to a minimum.

When he was one hundred yards west of the training camp, Clint turned north, heading toward a point parallel to the entrance. The tower guard would be facing the road, which would put Clint to his immediate left and within his eyes' peripheral vision. Stealth would be required.

Moving slowly and quietly now, as sound would travel easily to the tower, he looked for a location to mount the camera. Seeing a grouping of scrub nested around a jagged boulder, and judging it to be an ideal place for the camera, he began a slow, stealthy approach.

A snap sound came from the tower and a powerful search lamp was illuminated. The guard began panning the road slowly and then over to the barren expanse where Clint had dropped to the ground, blending with the environment as best he could. If he was seen, he would die as he was within easy range of the tower's machine gun.

The spotlight panned directly over him, but continued on, only to pan back over him again before the switch's snap was heard again and darkness prevailed. Clint had turned his head away from the spotlight to prevent a reflection from his eyes, but now turned to see the dimming filament. It was mounted to the tower roof, hidden from casual view. I wonder what other surprises we might encounter, he thought.

Clint then belly-crawled the rest of the way to the rock. He estimated he had only ten minutes until the charge ignited the fuel shack, so he began setting up the camera quickly. Embedding the camera shaft into the ground behind the rock and elevating the camera an inch above the rock was fast work. Activating the camera and using the handheld monitor, he adjusted the angle and zoom and then fine-tuned the focus on the gate to the training camp. Satisfied, he slowly headed further west, away from the camp, reaching a safe distance began running.

When he was about five hundred yards due west of the camp, the fuel shack exploded. Clint turned and crouched to see a fireball rising hundreds of feet into the air. The entire training camp was illuminated as if in daylight, and he could hear shouts of alarm coming from within the camp. The diversion was activated and he prayed it would draw Farooq out.

Clint now headed due north in a comfortable trot toward the Euphrates, knowing he was out of sight range. Another explosion shook the ground beneath his feet and turning, he saw a fuel drum rocket into the sky, the first of many.

The Black Hawks has arrived at the landing zone without being detected. The F470 Combat Rubber Raiding Crafts were secured in the Euphrates while the team checked their weapons. The Black Hawks had already retreated to their secluded layover location, about thirty miles south.

Meceli checked their communications channel, asking each to respond in the predetermined sequence. The sequence completed, she was alarmed to hear Clint check in as well.

"Clint, it is good to hear your voice!"

"Better to hear yours! The diversion went live about twenty minutes ago. The camera is placed and I am nearing the river."

"We are departing the landing zone now and will be at the bridge in fifteen," Meceli replied.

"See you there. Out."

The CRCCs were powered by seventy-five horse power Mercury outboard motors that had been modified for near-silent running. Everything was painted matt black to both prevent reflection and to blend with the river. They were serpents swimming silently upriver.

Life along the Euphrates was quiet, with fishermen fast asleep preparing for an early morning. There were few homes and buildings near the river, and the few there were dark.

At the halfway point, a single high-intensity light was seen approaching them at speed from downriver. TJ called for the CRCCs to navigate into a semi-secluded area where a tree had fallen partially into the river. The outboard engines were stopped as they waited for the craft to appear, ready for assault if they were detected.

As it came closer to their location, TJ could see the craft was a modified cabin cruiser with a search light and a machine gun mounted on the foredeck. A patrol boat, he concluded, but it was not picked up in any of their reconnaissance. He wondered if this was a one-time recon or if the craft was moving to another location.

The patrol boat continued moving downriver and passed them without notice. TJ ordered the CRCC pilots to wait for his order before restarting the outboards and continuing on to the bridge. When the craft had made the turn and was out of sight, he gave the order to move.

***

Clint had arrived at the bridge and then moved closer to the river to greet Meceli, TJ, and the team when they arrived. He was happy to see the road empty of cars and trucks, just as Amatullah had predicted.

As he hydrated, his thoughts moved to timing. It was now a few minutes' shy of 2400 hours, and the diversion had started about ninety minutes before. He expected, if it had worked, that Farooq would be crossing the bridge very soon. He prayed that it had worked; his intuition told him it had.

Clint heard the subtle hum of the CRCCs' outboards just as they beached, and watched as the team secured the rubber rafts and began to deploy.

Touching his comm button, he said, "I am twenty yards due south of you. Everything is clear."

Meceli reached his location first and threw herself into his arms, "You look no worse for the wear, Clint!"

"Did anyone ever tell you that you are very intimidating with your face blackened like that?"

"You better watch yourself, big man," she said with a chuckle.

Breaking their embrace, Clint offered TJ his hand in welcome. "Any troubles?"

"Nice to see you, Clint. Yeah, a patrol boat…but it passed us by."

Clint then greeted each of the team by name—Hawkeye, OJ, Ben, Dicky, Al, and Mick, and was pleased to see them all alert and ready for action. Truth be told, he expected nothing less.

Meceli broke the reunion, "Guys, headlights approaching the bridge. Multiple vehicles."

They all broke for suitable cover and watched as three vehicles proceeded across the bridge. When they were parallel to their location, Clint marked a technical followed by a black Mercedes sedan, followed by a technical. Farooq had taken the bait.

Clint pulled out the handheld flat-screen monitor and placed it for everyone to see. The high-resolution camera showed the training camp entrance with the gates closed and no activity. The fuel shed was still burning and added light to the compound.

While they waited for the vehicles to reach the gate, Clint explained the diversion and his killing of the training leader.

About ten minutes later, the convoy of vehicles reached the now-open gates. "Okay. Let's get our welcome party ready for their return, TJ."

"You got it, boss. Hawkeye and OJ, take up your sniper positions. Ben, you and Dicky lay the spike strips on the roadside, and be sure they are oriented for the return vehicles. When the vehicles leave the camp, I will signal you to pull them across the road. Al and Mick, activate the cell phone jammer and take your positions on the east and west sides of the road. Wait for my go as the vehicles return. Go!"

Now they waited.

CHAPTER TWENTY-TWO: SUNDAY

How long Farooq would stay in the training camp was unknown. Clint believed that he would personally review the damage and likely discipline the camp leaders. Would the dead body lead him to believe that the fire was started by the brutal camp leader, perhaps a smoking accident? Clint concluded that Farooq would stay maybe an hour before he sought the comforts of his al-Raqqah home.

Clint had dimmed the intensity of the flat-screen, both to conserve battery and to reduce the impact on his night vision. He watched it closely, knowing they would have no more than ten minutes to allow the team to get ready once the vehicle convoy left the camp.

Meceli and TJ watched the screen as intently as Clint. They were rewarded at 0115 hours, as the convoy pulled through the gate. A fourth vehicle had joined the convoy at the rear.

"Damn!" TJ said. "We prepared for this, Clint. I have my Barrett XM109 with 25mm cargo rounds. I will take out the additional technical."

"Glad you thought of bringing that cannon, TJ," Clint said.

TJ then alerted the team, "Four vehicles just left the compound. Ben and Dicky, lay the spike strips and the get into your positions. I will take out the last technical. Wait for my go."

TJ took off at a run to get into position, while Clint and Meceli left to their positions closer to where Farooq's Mercedes was expected to stop. Clint had his pack with the magnetic puck and putty to break into Farooq's armored Mercedes.

Minutes passed with the team in place and at the ready. The convoy could now be seen and heard. Each technical had a man standing behind the machine gun in the pickup truck's bed. They were traveling at about forty miles per hour, and would hit the spike strips in less than thirty seconds.

TJ yelled, "Go!"

Small explosions were heard as the front technical's tires blew out. The driver was caught unaware. Struggling to keep the vehicle on the road, he swerved to the right and turned over, rolling twice before coming to a stop. It was out of the fight.

The Mercedes' tires blew next and was in better control, sliding sidewise but staying on the road. The second technical's tires blew and was unable to stop, broadsiding the Mercedes. The machine gun operator was thrown to the bed of the pickup but righted himself quickly. He swung the machine gun looking for targets before Hawkeye placed a round in his head.

The last technical had four good tires and had stopped. The machine gunner looked for targets as OJ's round severed his head from his body.

TJ then sent several rounds from his cannon into the cab of the third technical, but not before the driver and passenger had bailed out.

The occupants remained in the Mercedes as Clint had expected. But the second and third technical had drivers and passengers that had spilled from the vehicles and were taking up positions to repel the attack. With no targets in sight, they were firing wildly. That was their mistake as it marked their positions for OJ and Hawkeye, who took two of them out within seconds.

The other two had better positions, shielded between the two technicals. One had a clear view of Meceli, who lay partially hidden by a small boulder. He started rapid firing, the illuminated tracer helping him zero in on her position.

Clint, seeing that Meceli would be hit in seconds, ran through the fire, diving at the end to get a bead on the shooter. He rolled to a stop and in a single fluid motion, raised his weapon and fired a short burst, each round finding its mark.

Hawkeye had moved thirty yards to the north and found the back of the last shooter. Two rounds silenced him.

TJ then ordered a sweep, "Al and Mick, secure the area!"

Clint and Meceli then approached the Mercedes from the rear to prevent Farooq's men from opening a window and shooting.

Meceli covered Clint's back as he climbed over the Mercedes' trunk, placed the puck on the roof, and pulled the lever. By the time he had climbed down, Ben and Dicky had taken defensive positions on the right and left side of the Mercedes.

This freed Meceli to place the long rope-like putty strip around the passenger-side door. She then struck the end with her combat knife and it ignited like a sparkler.

Hawkeye and OJ made their way back to the rest of the team, waiting for the putty to complete its burn around the door's circumference.

TJ took control, "Hawkeye, OJ, Al, and Mick, make ready the CRCCs. We will be there in minutes."

The putty had done its job and the door literally fell from the Mercedes' body. Clint, Meceli, and TJ held weapons pointed at the interior but there was no movement. The driver, front and rear passenger, and Farooq were unconscious.

Clint pulled Farooq out by his arms, dragging him a few feet away from the car. TJ leaned into the Mercedes and, using his side arm, put a bullet into the heads of the driver and both passengers.

Clint handed his rifle to TJ and then lifted Farooq onto his shoulder in a fireman's carry, heading toward the CRCCs in a trot. Meceli and TJ followed.

While making their way to the river, TJ alerted the Black Hawks that they would be at the extraction point in twenty minutes.

Once in the CRCCs and making their way to the extraction point, TJ ordered Ben to zip tie Farooq's arms and legs and gag him, as a precaution should he recover from the gas the puck had injected into the Mercedes' cabin.

They made it to the extraction point without incident, minutes before the Black Hawks landed. The CRCCs were scuttled and found their way to the bottom of the Euphrates.

Once in the air, Clint used the Black Hawk's secure radio to update Cole. "Cole, Operation Mandan complete. No casualties. Package alive."

The first order of business once back on the *Eisenhower* was the operational debrief. Cole and Director Douglas were on video conference and the entire team was present.

The director led the debrief and was exceptionally pleased with the results. "TJ, very well done. And I can see your team is in the room as well. You should all know that what you accomplished will shorten the fight with ISIS and al-Qaeda. Thank you for your service, men!"

He continued, "Clint and Meceli, flawless planning and execution, well done!"

Clint said, "Mr. Director, we are not done yet." His tone was far more demanding than typical; driven by his disgust of the brutality he had witnessed from the camp's leaders.

"Explain. Clint?" the director asked, accepting the unusually harsh tone.

"The training camp isn't exactly what we thought. The children are captives and being brutalized by the camp leaders. The walls are to keep the children from escaping. Now that we have had an eyes-on recon, I suggest that we take out the leaders' quarters and the guard tower. It can be done by drone with no risk of collateral damage. And I suggest we do it this evening."

"I will make that happen, Clint."

The President of the United States, William Thurston Covey, looked into the camera from behind his desk in the Oval Office.

Good evening, my fellow Americans. I have additional news to share with you as we close out the threat the press has named, 'ISIS in America'. This past week, the last ISIS cell was neutralized by Collaborative counter-terrorism operatives, right here in Washington D.C. There were two American casualties. In parallel with that operation, the Collaborative located and neutralized the ISIS training camp located west of Missoula, Montana, in the Lolo National Forest. There were no American casualties.

I am very happy to inform you that there are no ISIS cells operating on American soil. I know that you join me in congratulating Director Douglas and the entire Collaborative team on their rapid success to keep the American people safe.

We have learned a great deal over the past two weeks about how ISIS operates, their funding sources, and their strategies. I have labored over keeping secret what I will now share, but believe each American has a right to know—a need to know.

As you know, on May 2, 2011, Osama bin Laden, the founder and head of the Islamist terrorist group al-Qaeda, was killed in Pakistan. His death created a void in the al-Qaeda leadership from which we believed they had never recovered. ISIS grew to fill that void, building their reputation through brutality and publicity. We now know that is only part of the story.

Farooq Abboud, an exiled wealthy Saudi Arabian living in al-Raqqah, Syria, had a different strategy. He was the Kingdom of Saudi Arabia's former Deputy Minister of Energy, exiled because he skimmed nearly one hundred million dollars into his private accounts. He was also a former Saudi Army special forces operative, and an Oxford graduate. A smart and dangerous man who professed the perverted radical views of Islam.

Farooq Abboud's strategy was to rebuild al-Qaeda, but do so in the shadows while the free world focused on eliminating ISIS. He actually invested his own great wealth to increasing the ISIS awareness, which in turn, kept the worlds eyes off al-Qaeda. It was actually his operatives, posing as ISIS, that we neutralized over the past two weeks.

But, we couldn't stop there. To keep America safe, we took the war to him in al-Raqqah, Syria. Less that twenty-four hours ago, Farooq Abboud was captured and his leadership team neutralized by Collaborative operatives. We have secured his bank accounts, preventing further investment in terrorism.

Abboud is a brutal radical terrorist. He imprisoned nearly one hundred girls and boys, training them in the ways of terror; brain washing them with radical views. These children had little choice as noncompliance would result in the deaths of their entire family. Hours ago, we neutralized the camp's leadership and watched as these children escaped back to their families. I have ordered the release of the drone video so that the free world can see there were no civilian casualties—none.

My fellow Americans, we have made significant progress in combatting terror over the past two weeks. But our work is not done. In a world where a single radical with an assault rifle can inflict massive carnage, each American must play a role. Be present. Be aware. Report unusual behavior to authorities immediately. Understand that our war is with radical Islamic terrorists, not with Islam and not with Muslims. Islam is a religion of peace.

Know that several Muslims helped the Collaborative achieve success over the last weeks, and we are deeply indebted for their help.

Thank you, and God bless America.

Clint and Meceli watched the president's national address, sipping a beer while sitting at the quiet bar of Alfonso's, located near the center of Washington D.C. They were both physically exhausted after their two-week ordeal, but were overcome with the need to be with one another.

The maître d' approached Clint, "Your table is ready, sir."

They pushed away from the bar, stood, and found each other's eyes; time stopped, emotions bubbled to the surface and love warmed their souls.